'It was like walking along the knife-edge of the highest possible mountain range, seeing life on one side and death on the other in the form of two deep, gorgeous and gleaming seascapes . . .'

LEONID ANDREYEV
Born 1871, Oryol, Russia
Died 1919, Finland

'Seven Hanged' was first published in Russia in 1908.

LEONID ANDREYEV

Seven Hanged

Translated by
Anthony Briggs

PENGUIN BOOKS

PENGUIN CLASSICS

UK | USA | Canada | Ireland | Australia
India | New Zealand | South Africa

Penguin Classics is part of the Penguin Random House group of companies
whose addresses can be found at global.penguinrandomhouse.com.

Penguin
Random House
UK

This edition published in Penguin Classics 2016
001

Translation copyright © Anthony Briggs, 2016

Set in 9/12.4 pt Baskerville 10 Pro
Typeset by Jouve (UK), Milton Keynes
Printed in Great Britain by Clays Ltd, St Ives plc

A CIP catalogue record for this book is available from the British Library

ISBN: 978-0-241-25213-0

www.greenpenguin.co.uk

To Leo Tolstoy

1. AT ONE O'CLOCK, SIR

The minister was a big fat man prone to apoplexy, so, to avoid unhealthy excitement, all possible precautions were taken before he was warned of a very serious attempt on his life that was being planned. Once the minister had been seen to take this news in his stride, even managing a smile, they gave him the details. The attempt was scheduled for the following morning, when he would be going out in his carriage to deliver his report: a number of terrorists, denounced by an informer and now under round-the-clock police surveillance, were due to meet up at one o'clock, armed with bombs and revolvers, and to wait for him to come out of the front entrance. That was where they would be arrested.

'Hang on,' said the minister in some surprise. 'How could they know that I'll be going out with my report at one o'clock, when *I* didn't know about it until just the other day?'

The Chief of Police spread his hands in bemusement. 'It's at *one o'clock*, sir.'

The minister shook his head, partly nonplussed, partly to acknowledge the good police work, and his dark, thick lips twisted into a sardonic smile, a smile that stayed on his face as he hurried to get out of the way of the police by following their instructions, which were to pack a few things and go off and spend the night in some hospitable mansion away from home. His wife and two children were also relocated away from the dangerous house where the bomb-throwers were due to meet up the next day.

With the lights burning in the borrowed mansion and welcoming familiar faces all around him, with much bowing and scraping, accompanied by smiles and expressions of indignation, the mandarin experienced a pleasant feeling of uplift, as if he had just received, or was about to receive, a great honour that had not been anticipated. But soon the people drove away to their various destinations, the lamps were put out and a stream of bright light flowed in from the electric streetlights through the plate-glass windows, looking lacy and spooky as it settled on the walls and ceiling. Penetrating intrusively into a house filled with pictures, statues and a silence also brought in from outside, this light, although gentle and hazy in itself, gave rise to uneasy feelings about the futility of bolts, fences and walls. And then, in the night-time stillness and solitude, in an unfamiliar bedroom, the mandarin was overcome by an unbearable feeling of dread.

A martyr to kidney trouble, he had found that any sudden agitation soon had his face, hands and feet bloated with water, the effect of which was to make him seem bigger, fatter and bulkier than ever. And now, lying there, a heap of swollen flesh weighing down the squashed bedsprings, he felt like a suffering patient, hurting all over, with a swollen face that didn't seem to belong to him, and he couldn't stop thinking about the cruel fate that some people had had in store for him. One after another he recalled all the recent atrocities when people of his standing, or even higher rank, had had bombs thrown at them, bombs that had torn bodies to shreds, spattered brains down dirty brick walls, and torn out teeth by the roots. And these memories had made his own fat and sickly body, now stretched out across the bed, seem like someone else's, having taken the full blazing impact of the explosion. His arms seemed to have been torn out at the shoulders, his teeth had been scattered, his brain tissue atomized, while his legs had gone numb and he lay there, toes up, like a corpse. He made a huge effort to stir himself, gasped out loud, and gave a good cough to make himself as uncorpse-like as possible. Snuggling down into the rustling bedclothes, vibrating with jangling springs, and determined to show the world that he was very much alive – nowhere near dead, miles away from death just like anyone else – he spoke out into the silence and loneliness of the bedroom with a deep staccato growl. 'Good lads! Well done, lads! Well done!'

It was his way of praising the detectives, policemen, soldiers and other men guarding his life, who had so cleverly prevented his assassination with their timely intervention. But, however much he stirred himself, praised his men, skewed his mouth into a forced grin of contempt for the stupid terrorists – miserable failures! – he still couldn't quite believe in his salvation. He wasn't sure that life wouldn't slip away from him, suddenly, any minute now. The death that those people had planned for him, which existed only in thought and intention, seemed to be still there, and it was going to stay there, it wouldn't go away until they were caught, stripped of their bombs and dumped in a dungeon. There it was, death, lurking in the corner, not going away, not allowed to go away, like a soldier placed on guard duty under orders from above.

'At one o'clock, sir.'

The familiar phrase rang out in a deluge of different voices, voices of gleeful contempt, rage, pig-headedness, meaningless noise. It was as if hundreds of wind-up gramophones had been installed in the bedroom, and all of them, one after another, were belting out what they had been programmed to say, with the single-minded stupidity of a machine.

'At one o'clock, sir.'

And that time, tomorrow's 'one o'clock', which until recently had been no different from any other time, nothing more than hands gliding around the dial of a gold watch, had now assumed an ominous authority, hopped off the dial and taken on a life of its own, growing into a great black partition which had divided his entire life in two. It was as if there had been no other time before or after, just this one time, strutting with bare-faced arrogance, the only time that had any right to a special existence of its own.

'What's that? What do you want?' raged the minister through clenched teeth.

A roar came from the gramophones.

'At one o'clock, sir.' And the black partition gave a grin and a bow.

Gritting his teeth, the minister sat up in bed with his head in his hands. He wasn't going to get to sleep, for sure, not on a ghastly night like this.

With a rising sense of clarity and horror, burying his face in his podgy, perfumed hands, he imagined himself getting up in the morning, in complete ignorance, having a cup of coffee, still in ignorance, and then putting on his outdoor things in the hall. Neither he, nor the porter handing him his fur coat, nor the servant still serving coffee, none of them would be aware that there was no point in drinking coffee or putting a coat on when in a few seconds all of this – the coat, his body and the coffee inside it – would be blasted to bits, taken away by death. Look, there's the porter opening the glass door . . . And that man, the nice, kind, polite porter, with his bright blue soldier's eyes and a chest full of medals, he, with his own hands is opening the terrible door, opening it because he is still in ignorance. And all of them smiling because of their ignorance.

'Oho!' he boomed suddenly, taking his hands from his face.

And then, peering ahead into the deep darkness with a firm, fixed stare, he reached forward, found a switch and put the light on. Then he got to his feet and, ignoring his slippers, walked barefoot across the carpet, taking in the unfamiliar bedroom until he found another knob and switched on a wall-light. It was now nice and light, only the rumpled bed with a blanket fallen to the floor bearing witness to a horror that had still not quite run its course.

In his night-clothes, with his beard all matted from the tossing and turning and his eyes full of anger, the mandarin looked like any other angry old man kept awake by insomnia and asthma. He had been stripped naked by the death that those people had planned for him; this had torn away the magnificence and imposing splendour which normally enveloped him. It was hard to believe that he wielded so much authority, and that this body of his, such a straight-forward, run-of-the-mill human body, was destined for a horrible death, to be destroyed in the bang and blaze of a monstrous explosion. Without getting dressed and impervious to the cold, he sat down in the first armchair that came to hand, rested his tangled beard on one hand, and stared up at the decorated plaster on the unfamiliar ceiling with a look of deep concentration and gentle wistfulness.

So, that's it then! That's what made him so scared and worried! That's why that thing lurks in the corner, and won't, can't, go away!

'Stupid fools!' he said, with contempt and strong feeling.

'Stupid fools!' he repeated in a louder tone, turning slightly towards the door so that he could be heard by anyone whom it might concern. Yes, the involvement was shared by the very people he had just referred to as good lads, the ones who, in their boundless enthusiasm, had told him every last detail of the assassination attempt.

'Of course!' he thought, suddenly struck by a strong idea that had come effortlessly into his mind. 'Now that I know about it – because they've told me everything – I feel terrified. But for them I would have been kept in ignorance, and I would have drunk my coffee with an easy mind. Of course, there's still death to deal with – but am I all that scared of death? I do have this kidney problem, and I'll have to die one day, but I'm not terrified, because my life goes on in ignorance. And those idiots kept saying, "At one o'clock, sir." Stupid fools! They thought I would be delighted, whereas *That Thing* lurks in the corner and won't go away. It won't go away because it's me thinking. And it's not death that is terrifying, only my knowing about it. And it would be totally impossible to live if a man were to know with complete certainty the date and time when he was sure to die. And all I get from those idiots is that warning: "At one o'clock, sir."'

He was suddenly aware of a nice sensation, a pleasant uplift, as if someone had told him he was immortal in every way, and was never going to die. And, with a renewed sense of himself as a man of strength and intelligence standing out from that herd of stupid fools who were making such a senseless and brazen incursion into the mystery of the future, he found himself contemplating the bliss of not knowing things, though he did so with the weary thought processes of a sickly old man who has seen it all. Nothing that lives, neither man nor beast, is allowed to know the date and time of his death. Only recently he had been ill; the doctors had told him he was going to die and he ought to make his final arrangements. But he didn't believe them, and, sure enough, he had remained alive. And something similar had happened when he had been young: his life was going nowhere, and he decided to commit suicide. He got a revolver ready, wrote his last letters, and even fixed the time of his death – but at the last moment he had thought better of it. At the last moment, anything can change, something completely unexpected can turn up, and this means that no one can ever tell himself when he is going to die.

'At one o'clock, sir.' That's what those kind-hearted asses had told him, and although they only told him because the death had already been prevented, the knowledge of its possible timing had been enough to fill him with horror. It was quite feasible that he could be killed one day, but it wouldn't happen tomorrow – no, not tomorrow – he was immortal, and he could sleep easy. Stupid fools, they had no idea of the great law they had subverted, of the abyss they had opened up, by saying, with such idiotic kind-heartedness, 'At one o'clock, sir.'

'No, not at one o'clock, sir; we don't know when. No, we don't know when. What's that?'

'Nothing.' An answer from the darkness. 'Nothing.'

'No. You were saying something.'

'Nothing. Nothing that matters. What I say is – tomorrow at one o'clock.'

And with a sharp sinking feeling, he realized there would be no sleep, rest or joy for him until that damned dark hour filched from the watch-face had gone by. Of the knowledge to be gleaned by no living creature only a shadow remained, standing in the corner, but it was enough to blot out the light and swamp a man with the impenetrable darkness of horror. The fear of death, once aroused, had spread all over his body, got into his bones, and it peeped out, pale-faced, at every pore.

Now it wasn't tomorrow's assassins that scared him – they had gone, disappeared into oblivion, merging into the host of enemies and hostile forces besetting his human existence – what he feared was something swift and inexorable: an apoplectic fit, a heart attack, a silly, skinny artery like the aorta suddenly giving way to blood-pressure and rupturing like a tightly stretched glove on bloated fingers.

He was horrified by his own short, fat neck, and he couldn't stand the sight of his stubby, podgy fingers or the shock of realizing how short they were and how they were filled with deadly moisture. And if, earlier on in the darkness, he had felt the need to stir himself in order to seem uncorpse-like, now, in this horribly cold and hostile brightness, it seemed terrifyingly impossible to move a muscle and reach for a cigarette or ring for assistance. His nerves were on edge, and every nerve seemed like a taut wire standing on end, topped by a tiny head with eyes staring in horror and a gaping mouth twitching in spasms and soundlessly gasping. He had no means of breathing.

And suddenly, down below in the darkness, in all the dust and cobwebs, an electric bell came to life somewhere up on the ceiling. A little metal clapper whirred in a spasm of horror against the rim of an echoing cup; then it stopped, then it rang again in a solid stream of jangling horror. It was Sir, ringing from his room.

Servants ran in. In some places among the chandeliers and on the walls some of the lamps lit up, not enough to provide light, but enough to allow shadows. They spread themselves everywhere, rising up in corners and crawling out across the ceiling, clinging tenuously to every protuberance and sticking to the walls. You couldn't tell where they had been before, these silent shadows, ugly and uncountable, the voiceless souls of voiceless objects.

A deeply resonating bass voice spoke out loud and clear. Then they telephoned for a doctor. Sir was feeling poorly. Sir's wife was also sent for.

2. SENTENCE: DEATH BY HANGING

It all worked out as the police had anticipated. Four terrorists – three men and one woman – armed with bombs,
infernal machines and revolvers, were seized outside the
entrance, and a fifth was discovered and arrested in the
conspirators' flat, she being the landlady. They also seized
a large quantity of dynamite, some semi-charged bombs and
other weapons. All those arrested were very young; the eld-
est of the men was twenty-eight years old, the younger
woman was only nineteen. Their trial took place in the same
fortress where they had been imprisoned after arrest; it was
summary justice conducted in secret, the way they did
things in those merciless times.

In court, all five behaved calmly; they were very
serious-minded and very thoughtful. So great was their contempt for the judges that none of them wanted to put on a
show of heroics with an uncalled-for smile or a false display
of triumphalism. Their calmness was balanced against a
need to shield their souls, and the great darkness about to
descend upon them in death, from the vile, intrusive gaze
of outsiders.

Sometimes they refused to answer; on other occasions
their answers were laconic, matter-of-fact and strictly rele-
vant, as if directed not at the judges but at the keepers of
statistics so that special forms could be filled in. Three of
them, one woman and two men, gave their real names, and
two refused to name themselves, thus remaining unknown
to the judges. And towards everything that went on in the

court they displayed the kind of curiosity that is diluted by emerging through a misty haze typical of people who are either seriously ill or obsessed by one huge, all-consuming idea. They would look up suddenly to catch an unusually interesting word as it flew past, and then go back to where their thoughts had been interrupted.

Nearest to the judges stood one of the accused who had given his name as Sergey Golovin, the son of a retired colonel, himself a former officer. He was still a young man, blond and stocky, so full of good health that neither imprisonment nor the prospect of imminent death could wipe the bloom off his cheeks or take the youthful expression of naïve happiness out of his light-blue eyes. He never stopped plucking at his scruffy blond beard, which he had not yet grown used to, and he stared fixedly out of the window, narrowing his eyes and blinking.

This was taking place at the end of winter, when, between the snowy blasts and the days of fog and frost, the approaching spring was sending out a herald in the form of a clear, warm, sunny day, or even a single hour, so spring-like and radiant with the greedy passion of young life that the sparrows in the street went wild with joy, and people seemed almost intoxicated. And today, through the top window, uncleaned and accumulating dust since last summer, an unusually beautiful sky could be seen. At first glance it seemed to consist of a milky-grey, smoky haze, but on closer examination the eye could make out a brighter blue beginning to shine through, deeper, sharper and ever more boundless. And by revealing itself gradually, with its purity veiled in a cloud of mist, it seemed as winsome as a young girl and as easy to fall in love with. And Sergey Golovin squinted up at that sky through his long, fluffy eyelashes, first with one eye then the other, while pulling at his little beard and looking deeply preoccupied. On one occasion, his fingers jerked and his face screwed itself into a spasm of childish delight, but a glance around the court was enough to extinguish this like a spark underfoot. Almost immediately a change came over the redness in his cheeks; without really turning pale, they took on an earthy, deathly shade of grey and his white-tipped fingers twisted bits of his fluffy hair, painfully torn out by the roots, in a vice-like grip. Nevertheless, the joy of living and of springtime won through, and within minutes his young, ingenuous face was turned up again towards the spring sky.

It was in the same direction, up at the sky, that the anonymous pale young girl with the pet-name of Musya also turned her eyes. She was younger than Golovin, but the severity of her manner and the black gleam in her proudly focused eyes gave her an older look. Only her soft and very slender neck and her no less slender girlish arms bore witness to her age, though there was also an indefinable something about her, to do with youth itself, that rang out in her voice with true clarity of tone and the purest harmony, like a well-loved musical instrument tuned to perfection, adding musicality to the simplest of her words and exclamations. She looked pale, but it was not the pallor of death, it was that special flaming white heat that occurs when a huge great fire seems to have been lit inside a person so that their body glows with light from within as if it was shining through the finest Sèvres porcelain. She sat there scarcely moving a muscle; only now and then did a surreptitious movement betray the fingering of a circular mark on the third finger of her right hand, the trace of a ring recently removed. And she stared at the sky not from any tender feelings or happy memories but because, in this dingy hall of officialdom, that patch of blue sky was the most beautiful place, a realm of purity and truth that was not trying to winkle secrets out of her eyes.

Sergey Golovin had won the sympathy of the court; she was the one they hated.

Alongside her, the unidentified man known as Werner sat there equally unmoving, in a rather affected pose, hands folded between his knees. If you can slam a face like a thick door, the unidentified man had banged shut the iron door of his face and secured it with an iron padlock. He looked down at the dirty floorboards without stirring, and you couldn't tell whether he was calm or intensely agitated, whether his thoughts were miles away or he was concentrating on the police giving their evidence. He was a small man with noble features finely drawn. His winsome appearance and sensitivity brought to mind a moonlit night in some southern clime under shadowy cypresses at the seaside, yet he also evoked a sense of formidable inner strength, indomitable self-assurance, cold control and heroic will. On his lips the very politeness with which he gave his terse, measured responses, accompanied by a slight bow, had an ominous ring, and if the prison smock looked like a ludicrous joke on the other prisoners, on this man it was such an alien form of dress that it went completely unnoticed. And although the other terrorists had been caught in possession of bombs and infernal machines, Werner was seized with nothing more than a black revolver; for some reason the judges took him to be the leader and when they addressed him, they did so with a touch of deference, in a laconic, businesslike manner.

The next one along was Vassily Kashirin, a man totally obsessed by an excruciating fear of death, accompanied by an equally desperate desire to suppress this dread and keep it from the judges. Since early morning, when they had been brought before the court, his galloping heartbeat had left him scarcely able to breathe, permanent beads of sweat stood out on his forehead, his hands were just as sweaty yet also cold, and a cold, sweaty shirt stuck to his body, hampering his movements. With a supreme effort of will, he stopped his fingers from trembling, his voice remained firm and clear, and his eyes kept steady. He took in nothing of his surroundings, voices seemed to come at him through a fog, and back into the same fog he dispatched his desperate responses in an attempt to reply in strong, loud tones. But once he had responded, he immediately forgot what had been asked and how he had answered, and relapsed into a terrible, wordless struggle with himself. And death emanated from him so obviously that the judges avoided looking at him, and his age was as hard to guess as that of a dead body well into decay. According to his papers he was only twenty-three years old. Once or twice Werner gently nudged him on the knee, and each time he responded with a simple phrase. 'It's all right.'

The most terrible moments were when he felt a sudden urge to scream, to yell out with the desperate wordless cry of a wild beast. When this happened, he nudged up against Werner, who responded to him without looking up. 'It's all right, Vasya. Won't be long.'

Then came the fifth terrorist, Tanya Kovalchuk, who, despite her own agonizing despair, enfolded the others with a watching maternal eye. She had not yet had any children, being as young and rosy-cheeked as Sergey Golovin, but she seemed like a mother to them all; there was so much concern and limitless affection in her every glance, every smile and all her terror. She completely ignored the court as if it were a kind of sideshow; all she took in was the way they answered the questions – was that a tremor in the voice, is that a show of fear, does that one need a drink of water?

She was too anguished to look at Vasya; all she could do was wring her chubby fingers. She watched Musya and Werner with pride, admiration and a look of serious concentration on her face. She did her best to pass a smile over to Sergey Golovin.

'Dear boy, he's looking up at the sky. Go on, keep on looking up there, my darling boy,' she thought as she watched him. 'But, oh dear, Vasya. What is it, what's wrong with him? What can I do about him? I can't say anything. That would make things worse. It might make him cry.'

And like a still pond at dawn reflecting every passing cloud, her sweet, kind, chubby face reflected every quick movement and every thought coming from the four of them. The idea that she was also being judged and would also be hanged never crossed her mind, such was her profound indifference. It was in her rooms that the supply of bombs and dynamite has been discovered and, oddly enough, she had been the one to fire at the policemen, wounding one of them in the head.

It was getting on for eight o'clock when the court proceedings came to an end. The sky had gradually turned dark blue and faded before the eyes of Musya and Sergey Golovin, but instead of radiating the pink hue and gentle smile of a summer's evening, it just clouded over, getting greyer and greyer, and then suddenly it was all cold and wintry. Golovin heaved a sigh, stretched himself and glanced up at the window a couple of times, but there was nothing to be seen beyond the cold, dark night, so, still fingering his little beard, he turned like a curious child to have a good look at the judges and the soldiers with their guns, and he smiled across at Tanya Kovalchuk. As for Musya, when the sky faded, she avoided looking down at the floor and calmly transferred her gaze to a little cobweb in one corner that gently wobbled as warm air rose invisibly from the steam-heating system. She stayed like that until sentence was pronounced.

After the sentencing, the condemned men and women took leave of their frock-coated lawyers, avoiding eye contact with these pitifully distraught and guilt-ridden people before coming together briefly in the doorway to exchange a few remarks.

'It's all right, Vasya. Won't be long now,' said Werner.

'Yes, brother, I'm all right,' said Kashirin in a loud, calm voice, almost enjoying himself.

And indeed, his face took on a pinkish hue, no longer like that of a decaying corpse.

'Bugger them all, they've hanged the lot of us,' said Golovin, reduced to a simple curse.

'We had it coming to us,' came Werner's calm reply.

'Tomorrow they'll give formal pronouncement of the sentence, and we'll all be locked up together,' said Kovalchuk, reassuringly. 'We'll be together right up to the execution.'

Musya said nothing. Then she took a firm step forward.

3. NOT HANG ME

Two weeks before the terrorists' trial, different officials from the same regional military court had tried a peasant, Ivan Yanson, and sentenced him to death.

This man, Ivan Yanson, was a labourer employed by a wealthy farmer, virtually indistinguishable from all the other workmen in the local peasantry. He was Estonian by birth, from Wesenberg, and, after moving on from farm to farm over the years, he had ended up near the capital. He spoke very poor Russian, and since his master was a Russian, Lazarev by name, and there were no Estonians in the locality, he had hardly spoken a word for pretty well the past two years. Not that he seemed to have any desire for conversation. He didn't talk to people, but he didn't talk to the animals either; he kept quiet while watering or harnessing a horse, slowly and tentatively shuffling around it, and when the horse, disconcerted by the silence, started to play up and jump about, he would lay into it with a big whip, not saying a word. He would beat him viciously, with a cold and bitter determination, and if this was happening when he was roaring drunk, he would work himself up into a frenzy. Way back at the house you could hear the lashing whip and the staccato clatter of hooves from the scared and suffering animal as they echoed on the floorboards of the barn. The master would give Yanson a beating for having whipped the horse, but the Estonian proved incorrigible, so he gave up on him.

Once or twice a month Yanson got drunk, and this usually occurred on days when he drove the master to the big railway station, which had a bar. Having dropped the master off, he would drive out half a mile or so from the station, park the horse and sledge in some deep snow off the road, and wait patiently for the train to depart. The sledge would stand there, leaning to one side, almost recumbent, with the horse up to his belly in a snowdrift, legs splayed, occasionally nuzzling the soft, crunchy snow and licking at it, while Yanson sprawled awkwardly across the sledge, apparently dozing. The drooping ear-flaps of his tatty cap dangled down impotently like a setter's ears, and his little button-nose looked red and runny.

Then Yanson would go back to the station and lose no time in getting himself drunk.

He completed the return trip to the farm, a good seven miles, galloping flat-out. The shattered and terrified little horse ran itself into the ground, the sledge rocked all over the place, banking, bending and crashing against posts, while Yanson, who had dropped the reins and was in danger of flying out onto the road with every minute that passed, half-sang and half-yelled incoherently obscure bits of

Estonian. But more often than not, he didn't sing, he kept silent, gritting his teeth against an inscrutable upsurge of rage, pain and exuberance, and barrelled on, blind to oncoming traffic, without shouting out warnings or slowing down as he careered around bends or down slopes. How he avoided running somebody down or smashing himself to death during one of these mad chases is anybody's guess.

He should have been sacked long ago, as he had been from other jobs, but he came cheap and the other workers weren't much better, so he stayed on for two years. Yanson's life was one in which nothing ever happened. One day he received a letter written in Estonian, but, since he was illiterate and there weren't any other Estonian-speakers, the letter went unread, and in a spasm of savage, fanatical indifference, as if he had no idea that the letter might contain news from home, Yanson chucked it onto the manure heap. On one occasion, apparently lusting for a woman, Yanson tried it on with the cook, but he got nowhere; he was turned down and laughed at. He was a little runt of a chap with a sickly, spotty face and muddy-coloured eyes that looked sleepy and boozy. But Yanson took this setback on the chin, and made no more approaches to the cook.

But, although he didn't speak much, Yanson was always listening. He listened to the dreary snow-covered countryside with small pats of frozen manure looking like rows of little snowy graves, and the dark-blue distant haze and the humming telegraph poles and people talking to each other. What the countryside and telegraph poles spoke about was known only to him, but what people were saying to each other worried him: nothing but rumours – of murder, robbery and arson. And one night a special sound had been heard: in the next village a little church bell rang out with a thin, helplessly tinkling noise like that of a carriage-bell. Strangers had ridden up, pillaged the wealthy farm, murdered the owner and his wife, and set fire to the house.

And now anxiety was the rule, even on Yanson's farm. The dogs were allowed to run free not just at night-time but also by day, and at night the master slept with a gun at his side. He wanted to give Yanson the same kind of gun, an older version with only one barrel, but the Estonian twisted it in his hands and refused inexplicably to accept it. The master, at a loss to understand the reason for his refusal, cursed him up hill and down dale, but the reason was simple: Yanson had more faith in his Finnish knife than this rusty old thing.

'Be the death of me,' said Yanson with a sleepy look in his beady, glassy eyes.

The master threw up his hands in desperation. 'You're a stupid fool, Ivan. Can't do a damn thing with farmhands like you.'

And one winter night, when the other farmhand had been dispatched to the station, that same Ivan Yanson who didn't believe in having a gun had carried out a very complex attempt at armed robbery, murder and rape. The way he did it was surprisingly simple: he locked the cook in her kitchen and then, at his leisure, with the air of a man dead on his feet for lack of sleep, he approached the master from behind and stabbed him repeatedly in the back. The master collapsed unconscious, and the mistress ran around the room screaming, while Yanson, baring his teeth and brandishing his knife, began ransacking the trunks and chests of drawers. He found some money, and then, apparently noticing the mistress for the first time, he surprised even himself by making advances with every intention of raping her. But by now he had dropped the knife, and when the mistress turned out to be stronger than him, not only did she decline to be raped, she came near to throttling the life out of him. At this point, the master showed signs of stirring, the cook was banging away with the oven-fork in an effort to break the kitchen door down, and Yanson ran outside. He was caught within the hour, squatting in a corner of the barn and striking match after dead match in an attempt at arson.

A few days later the master died from blood-poisoning, and Yanson took his place in a queue of other robbers and murderers waiting to be tried and sentenced to death. In court he was the same as always: a puny little man with a spotty face and a sleepy look in his beady, glassy eyes. Somehow he didn't seem to fully grasp what was going on, and he looked totally indifferent; his white eyelashes blinked as his lifeless eyes took in the unfamiliar courtroom in all its pomp without registering any curiosity, and he picked his nose crudely with a stiff, horny finger. Only those who might have seen him in church of a Sunday could have guessed that he had made an attempt at smartening up for the occasion; he wore a dirty, red knitted scarf around his neck and he had dampened his hair down in a few places that looked smoother and lay down flatter than on the other side, where it curled up in thin, blond tufts like wisps of straw left behind on a scanty hail-blown meadow.

When the sentence was pronounced: 'Death by Hanging', Yanson was shaken. He blushed to the roots of his hair and began twisting the scarf off and on, as if it was throttling him. Then he waved his hands about crazily, pointed to the judge who had read out the sentence, and spoke to the judge who had not.

'She said to hang me.'

'Who is "she"?' came the deep voice of the presiding judge, who had read out the sentence.

There were smiles all round, hidden behind moustaches and court papers, but Yanson levelled his forefinger at the president, and scowled at him in an angry response. 'You!'

'Well?'

Yanson turned his eyes back to the unspeaking judge, who was struggling not to smile, in whom he sensed an ally, someone not party to the sentence, and he said again, 'She said to hang me. Not hang me.'

'Take the prisoner away.'

But Yanson had time to repeat what he had said, with grim determination. 'Not hang me.'

He looked so stupid, with anger written all over his little face, as he strove vainly to invest it with gravitas, and with his finger still pointing, that even the soldier escorting him broke the rules by speaking to him in a low voice as he walked him away. 'You're a stupid fool, laddie.'

'Not hang me,' Yanson persisted.

'Sorry, chum. You're getting strung up. No time to kick.'

'Hey, that's enough!' cried the other escort, incensed by this. But he gave in and couldn't help adding, 'You went out robbing. Why did you have to take a human life? Now you're going to hang.'

'Any chance of a pardon?' asked the first guard, beginning to feel sorry for Yanson.

'You what? Pardon the likes of 'im? Anyway, that's enough talking.'

But Yanson had already stopped talking. He was locked up in the same cell he had been in for the past month and had got used to, as before he had got used to getting beaten, drinking vodka and looking at the snowy fields with round hillocks like a cemetery. He even felt a surge of happiness when he saw his bed and his window grille, and when they gave him some food – not having eaten anything all day. The only nasty thing was what had gone on in court, but he couldn't think about that, he didn't know how to. Death by hanging was beyond his imagination.

Even though Yanson had been given a death sentence, there were lots of others like him; in that prison he wasn't seen as a special criminal. This meant that the staff talked to him without fear or respect, the way they talked to all the prisoners who hadn't been sentenced to death. It seemed as if his death wasn't really death at all. The head guard, when he heard what the sentence was, spoke as if he was teaching him a lesson.

'Well, brother. They've gone and hung you then!'

'When will they hang me?' asked Yanson cautiously.

The guard gave it a moment's thought. 'Well, brother, it's like this. You're going to have to wait while they gets a party of you together. They won't do it for one – especially one like you. They wants the numbers up.'

'But *when*?' Yanson insisted. It didn't offend him in the slightest that he wasn't worth hanging on his own, and he didn't believe it anyway. He thought it was a pretext for delaying the execution and then cancelling it altogether. He felt bucked by this. The uncertain and terrible moment that he couldn't begin to think about was moving steadily away into the distance, becoming as unlikely as a fairytale, no different from any other death.

'You go on and on about *when*,' said the guard in exasperation (he was a stupid and gloomy old man). 'It's not like hanging a dog. You don't just nip round the back of the shed, and that's it. Stupid fool, is that what you want?'

'I don't want at all!' Yanson scowled with pleasure. 'It was her what said to hang me. I don't want!'

And he gave a little laugh, perhaps for the first time in his life, a jarring, idiotic laugh that was strangely cheerful and enjoyable. Like a goose honking, 'haw, haw, haw!' The guard looked at him in amazement, then gave a grim scowl; this absurd display of cheeriness from a man who was due to be executed was an insult to the prison and to execution itself, and it turned them both into something weird. Suddenly, for one moment, a split second, the old guard who had spent all his life in that prison, for whom its laws were the laws of nature, saw that place, and life itself, revealed as a madhouse, with himself, the head guard, as the chief madman.

'Damn you! Fuck you!' said the guard. 'What are you grinning at? You're not in the pub now.'

'I don't want! Haw, haw, haw!' said Yanson, still laughing.

'Satan!' said the head guard, feeling the need to cross himself.

24

No one could have looked less like Satan than this man with his flabby little face, but there was something in his goosey honking that undermined the sanctity and strength of the prison. Let him go on honking a bit longer and you could see the walls crumbling away and the rusty grilles collapsing, and the chief guard leading the prisoners out through the gate . . . 'There you are, gentlemen, have a stroll around town, or maybe some of you would like to see the countryside?' Satan!

But by now Yanson had stopped laughing. He was left with a sly scowl on his face.

'All right. Watch it, then!' said the chief, with the vaguest of threats, and off he went, looking back over his shoulder.

All that evening Yanson was calm and you might even say cheerful. He kept on repeating the same phrase under his breath, 'Not hang me,' and it was so convincing, so full of wisdom, so incontrovertible, that there was nothing to worry about. His crime was long forgotten, except for the odd pang of regret for not having managed to rape the mistress. Soon he even forgot about that.

Every morning Yanson asked when he was going to be hanged, and every morning the chief gave the same angry response.

'It'll come, Satan, just you wait.' And off he would go as fast as he could before Yanson could burst out laughing again.

And because of these identically repeated words, plus the fact that each day got off to a start, proceeded on its way and came to an end like every other ordinary day, Yanson became totally convinced there wouldn't be an execution. It didn't take him long to put the court right out of his mind and for days on end he lay sprawling on his bed, his head full of vague but joyful dreams about the gloomy, snowy fields with their little hillocks, the station bar, and something beyond that, gleaming in the distance. In the jail he was well fed, and quicker than you might think, within only a few days, he had put on weight and begun to strut about the place.

'By now she would have been in love with me like this,' he thought, with the mistress in mind, 'I'm fattened out now, no worse than the master.'

What he did miss was a drink of vodka – a quick drink followed by a mad charge with the horse.

When the terrorists had been arrested, news of them reached the prison, and when Yanson asked his usual question, the chief gave a new response, sharp and unexpected. 'Won't be long now.'

His look was calm, and his speech heavy with meaning. 'Won't be long now. About a week, I'd say.'

Yanson's face paled, and his glassy eyes went cloudy as if he was nodding off as he spoke. 'You're joking?'

'You were the one who couldn't wait, and you're the joker. We are not allowed jokes. You like joking, but we are not allowed jokes,' said the chief guard in a lofty tone before walking away.

By the evening Yanson had shrunk down a little. His skin, which had been stretched and temporarily smoothed down, had now shrivelled into a mass of tiny wrinkles, and in some places it looked quite droopy. His eyes had become shrouded with sleep, and his every movement was slow and sluggish, as if each turn of the head, finger-movement or footstep was a complex and cumbersome procedure requiring a lot of careful forethought. At bedtime he lay down on his bunk without closing his eyes, and they stayed like that, open but sleepy, all night long.

'Aha!' said the chief with some satisfaction when he saw him next morning. 'See, me old darlin'. This ain't no pub.'

It was with the satisfied feeling of a scientist whose experiment has come out right again that he scrutinized the condemned man from head to toe. Now things would go the way they should. Satan had been put to shame, the sanctity of the prison and execution had been re-established, and now there was sympathy, even some genuine pity, in the way that the old man asked his questions.

'Do you want to see anybody? No?'

'What is this "see anybody"?'

'Well, just to say goodbye. Maybe your mother, or a brother?'

'Not hang me,' said Yanson in a soft voice, glancing sideways at the chief guard. 'I don't want.'

The guard took a look at him, and flung up a hand without saying another word.

By evening Yanson was a little calmer. The day had been such an ordinary one, the light from the cloudy winter sky had been so ordinary, the footsteps in the corridor and the animated talk had been so ordinary, and the sour smell of the cabbage soup had been so ordinary and so normal that once again he had ceased to believe in the execution. But as night came on, he began to feel terribly scared. Earlier on Yanson had treated night as nothing more than darkness, a particular period of blackness which you have to sleep through, but now he was aware of its essentially mysterious and ominous character. To avoid believing in death you must see and hear ordinary things around you: footsteps, voices, light, sour cabbage soup, and now everything was out of the ordinary. This silence and this darkness were in themselves akin to death.

And the more night dragged on, the more terrifying it became. With the naivety of a primitive creature or a child, who thinks all things are possible, Yanson felt like telling the sun to start shining. He begged and entreated the sun to do that, but night went on remorselessly, stretching its black hours out over the earth, and there was no force that could stop it in its course. And this impossibility, which had never before penetrated Yanson's feeble brain with such clarity, filled him with terror; without yet being fully aware of it, he was now sensing the proximity of death, and had placed one dying foot on the first step of the scaffold.

Daylight calmed him down again, but then the night filled him with horror, and things went along like this until the night when he saw sense and admitted the inevitability of death – in three days' time, in the early morning, at sunrise.

He had never thought about what it would be like to die, and he had no image of death, though now he could clearly sense – see and feel – that it had come into his cell to feel its way around and seek him out. And in an effort to save himself, he began running around the cell.

But the cell was so small it seemed to have no acute

angles, only obtuse ones, and he kept on being bounced back into the middle. And there was nothing to hide behind. The door was locked, and there was light. He said nothing as his upper body bumped into the wall several times and once banged against the door with a hollow clang.

He crashed into something, and fell to the floor face-down. It was now that he felt he was in *its* grasp. And as he lay there on his belly, clinging to the hard surface of the dark and dirty floor, Yanson gave a wail of terror. He lay there yelling at the top of his voice until they came to see to him. And even when they had picked him up, put him back on his bunk and poured cold water over his head, he still refused to open his rigidly closed eyes. When he half-opened one eye, all he saw was light in an empty corner and some-body's boot in the open space, and this set him off wailing again.

But the cold water began to do its work. He was also helped by the fact that the duty officer was the same old man as before, and he gave him a few medicinal slaps around the head. And this sensation of being alive did manage to dispel death, Yanson did open his eyes, and then he slept soundly through the rest of the night with his brain greatly befogged. He lay on his back with his mouth open and a lot of loud, melodious snoring. And the whites of his eyes shone with the smoothness of a deathly pallor through his partly closed eyelids.

And from now on everything in the world – day and night, footsteps, voices and sour cabbage soup – blurred into a single shock of horror, plunging him into a state of primitive bewilderment beyond comprehension. His feeble mind could not reconcile the two monstrous contradictions: the normality of daylight and cabbage soup versus the idea that tomorrow, or the day after, he was going to die. He thought of nothing, had no sense of time passing; he just stood there facing this contradiction in silent horror, with his brain split in two. And, because his face was its normal colour, neither paler nor redder than usual, he seemed to be at peace. Except that he had stopped eating and didn't sleep a wink. No, he spent the whole night either curled up on a stool, with his legs tucked timorously away, or creeping quietly around the room, with his sleepy eyes darting everywhere. His mouth hung half-open all the time, as if he was in a permanent state of extreme shock, and before picking up the simplest everyday object, he would give it a close, dull-witted scrutiny and accept it only with great reluctance.

And once he had become like this, the guard and the soldier deputed to watch him through the little grille began to ignore him. His behaviour seemed normal for a condemned man, and the chief guard likened it (without ever having had the experience himself) to the stunning of cattle by the butt of an axe prior to slaughter.

'He's been stunned. From now on until he dies, he won't feel a thing,' he would say, observing him with a seasoned eye. 'Can you hear me, Ivan? Eh? Ivan!'

'Not hang me,' came the lacklustre response from Yanson, again with a drooping jaw.

'If you hadn't murdered somebody, they wouldn't be hanging you,' said the chief guard, still a young man, but an imposing figure with a chestful of medals. 'You did the killing – now you don't want to be hung.'

'You wanted to kill, and get away with it. Stupid as hell, but damned clever.'

'I don't want,' said Yanson.

'All right, my friend. You carry on not wanting. It's up to you,' said the senior man indifferently. 'But you might be better off not talking nonsense, and sorting out your effects. Still things to be done.'

'He hasn't got any. Shirt and trousers, that's it. Oh, plus the fur cap. Quite a dandy with that!'

And so the time passed until Thursday. And then, at midnight on Thursday, a lot of people walked into Yanson's cell, and a gentleman wearing epaulettes spoke to him. 'Right. Get yourself ready. Time to go.'

Yanson, moving at his usual slow and weary pace, got dressed in everything he had, and finished by tying the dirty red scarf around his neck. As he watched him getting dressed, the same gentleman, cigarette in hand, said to somebody, 'Nice warm day, today. Real touch of spring.'

Yanson's tiny eyes were glued up, he was full of sleep and his footsteps dragged so stiffly that the guard spoke to him. 'Come on, get a move on. He's gone to sleep!'

Suddenly Yanson came to a halt. 'I don't want,' he said, weakly.

They grabbed him under the armpits and got him going; he took an obedient step forward, lifting his shoulders. Outside he was assailed by a springtime breath of moist air, and his little nose began to run. Although it was night-time, the thaw was underway and drops of water cascaded merrily from above, tinkling on the stones below. And as he waited for the policemen to get into the black, unlit carriage, stooping and jingling their swords, Yanson wiped his runny nose lazily with one finger and straightened his badly tied scarf.

4. US LADS FROM ORYOL

The same regional military court judges that had tried Yanson also sentenced another man to death by hanging, a peasant from Yeléts in the province of Orlov, by the name of Mikhail Golubets, better known as Gypsy Mike, and a Tartar by birth. His latest crime, proven beyond doubt, was the murder of three people in an armed robbery, but his murky career went far back into the mysterious depths of time. There were vague rumours of his implication in any number of other robberies and murders, and he had left behind him in his wake much blood and drunken depravity. He described himself as a villain quite openly and sincerely, though he could also be ironical, as when he claimed allegiance to those who called themselves, using the latest catchphrase, 'expropriators'. Seeing that denial would get him nowhere with his latest crime, he willingly confessed in detail, though when he was asked about his earlier career, he would do no more than bare his teeth, give a little whistle, and say, 'Look for the wind in the fields!'

But when they put him under pressure, Gypsy Mike struck an attitude of stolid and dignified concentration.

'Us lads from Oryol, we're all nutcases,' he would say in thoughtfully measured tones. 'Oryol lads is best. We can out-thieve the rest ... We're fathers and mothers – of all thieving brothers. But thieves from Yeléts – is the finest and best! Can't say fairer than that.'

He was called Gypsy Mike because of the way he looked and his constant thieving. He was ridiculously dark-haired and skinny, with spots of yellow sunburn on his high Tartar cheekbones; he had the look of a horse when he rolled the whites of his eyes, and he galloped around everywhere. His eyes didn't settle easily, but when they did, they were terrifyingly direct and eager to take things in; objects that he had glanced at seemed to lose something, transferring part of themselves to him and taking on a different character. A cigarette that had been no more than looked at by him became as repellent and disgusting to pick up as one that had been in somebody's mouth. A kind of permanent fretfulness lived inside him, twisting him like braided rope or sending him flying all over the place in a shower of whirling sparks. Even when he needed water, he drank it like a horse, almost by the bucketful.

In court he answered all questions by jumping to his feet and giving a straight response in the tersest terms.

'Right!'

Sometimes he added emphasis: 'Rrright!'

And once, quite unexpectedly, when the subject had moved on, he jumped up and addressed the president.

'Permission to whistle, sir!'

'What on earth for?' said the judge in surprise.

'They was giving evidence how I used to signal to my mates. This is how. Highly interesting.'

The president had his doubts, but permission was given.

Gypsy Mike lost no time in sticking four fingers in his mouth, two from each hand, and rolling his eyes in a frenzied glare. The lifeless atmosphere of the courtroom was pierced by a true wild-man bandit-whistle fit to deafen a horse, make it rear up on its haunches, and drain the colour from any human face. The desperate agony of a man being murdered, the savage thrill of a killer, a terrible pang of foreboding, a call for help, the darkness of foul weather in an autumn night, a sense of solitude – all of these things were there, in that shrieking, wailing sound, which belonged to neither man nor beast.

The president called out, and waved at Gypsy Mike, who obediently stopped his whistling. And like a solo singer who has triumphantly performed a difficult operatic aria which was always going to succeed, he took his seat, wiped his wet fingers down his smock and regarded his audience with an air of satisfaction.

'True villain!' said one of the judges, rubbing an ear.

But the other one, with a wide Russian beard and eyes no less Tartar-like than those of the defendant, cast a dreamy look into space above the gypsy's head, then gave a grin and a different response: 'That really was most interesting.'

And with easy hearts, without pity or any feelings of remorse, the judges sentenced Gypsy Mike to death.

'Right!' said Gypsy Mike when the sentence had been pronounced. 'Out in the open on a crossbeam. That's right!'

And, turning to his escort, he said with a young blade's bravado, 'Right. Let's go, misery-guts. Hang onto your gun, or I'll have it!'

The soldier glared, keeping a wary eye on him, exchanged

glances with his comrade and fingered the bolt on his gun. His opposite number did the same. And all the way back to the prison the soldiers seemed to be walking on air; totally absorbed in the criminal, they couldn't feel the ground under their feet, and they were oblivious to the passage of time or any sense of themselves.

Like Yanson, Gypsy Mike was to spend seventeen days in prison before execution. All seventeen passed so quickly – like a single day – in an inextinguishable dream of escape, freedom and life. The restless spirit that had taken over Gypsy Mike's personality was now contained within walls, grilles and a blank window, with nothing visible, and it had turned all its furious energy in on itself, burning his ideas away to nothing, like coals scattered across the floor. It was as if he was in a drunken stupor: a cloud of brilliant but half-formed images swarmed through his mind, jostling and blurring as they whirled past in a dazzling, unstoppable rush, all of them going in the same direction – towards escape, freedom and life. Some days Gypsy Mike would flare his nostrils like a horse and spend hours sniffing the air, imagining the smell of hemp and something burning with colourless, acrid smoke; sometimes he would spin around the cell like a top, feeling along the walls and tip-tapping with a finger, his eyes measuring distances, studying the ceiling, sawing through the bars. His jumpy behaviour worried the soldier on peephole duty, and several times, in despair, he threatened to shoot Gypsy Mike, who rounded on him with filthy words and jeering taunts. All this wrangling was settled peacefully only because it gradually degenerated into the kind of inoffensive rough-stuff between peasants in which any shooting would have been absurd and impossible.

Gypsy Mike got through his nights fast asleep, almost without stirring, in an ongoing state of dynamic immobility like a spring temporarily uncoiled. But once he was up on his feet he resumed the business of spinning around, weighing things up and groping about. His hands were invariably dry and hot, but sometimes his heart felt a flood of cold, as if an unmelting block of ice had been packed into his chest, giving him the dry shivers all over his body. At times like this, Gypsy Mike, already swarthy, turned black and took on the dark-bluish hue of cast-iron. And he formed a strange habit: as if he had eaten something excessively sweet and indigestible, he began licking his lips all the time, champing and spewing out the flow of saliva through his clenched teeth all over the floor. And he didn't finish what he was trying to say; his thoughts flashed past so quickly that his tongue couldn't keep up with them.

One afternoon the prison chief dropped in on him, accompanied by an escort. He took one look at the floor covered in spit, and spoke in gloomy tones. 'Huh. You've made a mess here.'

Gypsy Mike was quick to respond. 'You've messed up the whole world, and I've said nothing. What have you skulked in here for?'

The chief's gloomy tone did not change as he offered him the job of executioner.

Gypsy Mike grinned and laughed at him. 'Haven't you got one? Bloody marvellous! *You* do it. Ha, ha, ha! You've got necks and ropes, and nobody to do the hanging? By God, that's bloody marvellous!'

'You wouldn't have to die.'

'You bet I wouldn't. Dead men don't hang nobody. Stupid fool.'

'What about it? No difference to you one way or the other.'

'Anyway, how do you lot go about hanging people? I bet you smothers 'em on the quiet.'

'No, we do it to music,' snarled the chief.

'Stupid fool, course you got to have music. Like this?' And he let go with a rollicking song.

'Seem to have made your mind up,' said the chief. 'What's it to be? Let's have some sense out of you.'

Gypsy gave a grin. 'Hang on a minute! Go away, and come back. Then I'll tell you.'

At this point a new idea burst into the maelstrom of brilliant, though half-formed and dispiriting images that had flooded through Gypsy Mike's mind. Wouldn't it be nice to be an executioner dressed in a red shirt? He could see a vivid picture: a square thronged with people, a high scaffold and himself, Gypsy Mike, strolling up and down, complete with red shirt and axe. The sun cast its light on every head, giving the axe a cheerful glint, and radiating such richness and good cheer that even those who were having their heads chopped off had a smile on their faces. Just behind the people you could see carts and horses' muzzles – peasants in from the countryside – and, further away, the fields.

'Pfwah!' snorted the gypsy, slobbering and licking at his lips as he gobbed out a new stream of saliva.

But suddenly he felt as if a fur hat had been pulled over his head and yanked down right over his mouth. His eyes were going dim, he could hardly breathe and he felt that flood of cold in his heart, as if an unmelting block of ice had been packed into his chest, giving him the dry shivers again.

The chief called in a couple more times, but Gypsy Mike just grinned at him and said, 'Too soon. Come back again.'

Then, eventually, the chief flashed open the peephole and shouted in. 'You've had it now, dumb-cluck! Got somebody else.'

'Sod you. *You* hang 'em!' snapped the gypsy. And he put the idea of executing people out of his mind.

But towards the end, with the execution getting nearer, the rushing flood of broken images became too much to bear. The gypsy wanted to stop, he wanted to plant his feet wide apart and stop there, but the swirling maelstrom swept him away and, with everything swimming past, he had nothing to hold onto. And he was too upset to get any sleep; his dreams were different now, sharp-edged and bulking like coloured wooden blocks, still hurtling past faster than he could think. This was no longer a flow of water but a measureless torrent descending from a measureless height, swirling its way through the visible world of colour. When he had been free, Gypsy Mike had sported rather stylish moustaches and no other facial hair, but now he had grown a short, black, prickly beard which gave him a terrifyingly crazy look. Sometimes he would go berserk, wheeling right around his room without rhyme or reason, but still feeling his way over the rough-cast walls. And he still drank his water like a horse.

One evening, when the lights had been put on, he got down on all fours in mid-cell, and came out with a quavering howl like a wolf. As he did so, he looked deadly serious, as if his howling was a thing of vital importance. He would take in a good chestful of air and release it slowly in a long drawn-out quavering howl. He did this with his eyes screwed up tight and listening carefully to what was coming out. Even the trembling quality of his voice seemed rather calculated, and he seemed not to be making a senseless noise, but to be carefully composing every note of his wild animal howl and filling it with unspeakable terror and anguish.

Then, suddenly, he stopped howling and stayed where he was on all fours, without making another sound. Minutes passed, and then he started mumbling, breathing his words into the ground. 'My little chickens, lovely sweeties . . . My little chickens, lovely sweeties, let me off . . . Little chickens! Lovely sweeties! . . .'

And again he seemed to be listening carefully to the sounds as they came out. Saying a word and listening to it.

Then he jumped up and spent the next hour, without stopping for a breather, cursing and swearing in the filthiest language. 'Aargh! You lousy lot!' he yelled out, rolling his bloodshot eyes. 'Hanging's hanging, but not like . . . Aargh! You lousy lot!'

And the soldier, chalk-white and weeping with anguish and terror, banged on the door with his rifle-barrel and

39

screamed out helplessly. 'I'll shoot! By God, I'll shoot. Hear me?'

But he didn't dare shoot. Condemned prisoners were never shot at, unless there was a proper riot going on. Gypsy Mike gnashed his teeth and carried on swearing and spewing. His human brain, suddenly stuck on a razor-sharp life-and-death borderline, was crumbling like a lump of dried-out, weathering clay.

When they turned up in his cell during the night to take Gypsy Mike off to be executed, he shook himself and seemed to come back to life. He had a sweeter taste in his mouth and an unstoppable flow of saliva had welled up, but his cheeks took on a pinker tinge and his eyes sparkled with some of their old slyness and wild cunning. As he got dressed, he spoke to the official. 'Who's doin' the 'angin'? That new bloke? Won't have got his hand in yet, will 'e?'

'No need to worry about that,' said the official in a dry voice.

'Course I'm worried, your honour. It's me they're hangin', not you. Got plenty of government soap to hang us with?'

'All right. All right. That's enough from you.'

'You can see who's eaten all the soap,' said the gypsy to the superintendent. 'Look at his face. All shiny!'

'That's enough!'

'Give it plenty of soap!'

Gypsy Mike laughed at them, but the sweet taste in his mouth was building up, and suddenly his legs went all funny and numb. Still, he managed to call out as they walked outside. 'Carriage, please, for the Count of Bengal!'

5. KISS AND KEEP QUIET

The sentence passed on the five terrorists was pronounced in its final form and ratified on the same day. The condemned prisoners were not told when the execution would take place, but, judging by the way things usually went, they knew they would be hanged that night, or the next night at the latest. And when a meeting with relatives was proposed for the following day, Thursday, they knew that the execution was scheduled for Friday morning at dawn.

Tanya Kovalchuk had no relatives, and any that she did have lived miles away in the sticks, somewhere in Little Russia; they would be unlikely to know about the trial or the impending execution. Relatives were unthinkable for the unidentified Musya and Werner, which meant that only two of them, Sergey Golovin and Vassily Kashirin, were due for a family meeting. And both of them anticipated that get-together with a mixture of anguish and dread, though they could not refuse the old folk a final conversation and one last kiss.

Sergey Golovin was especially anguished by the prospect of meeting them. He loved his mother and father very dearly, he had spent time with them only recently, and now he was horrified that it had come to this. Execution itself, such an outrageous perversion with its demented potential to crush the human brain, was easier for his imagination to assimilate, and it seemed less terrifying, than those few short, incomprehensible minutes, which seemed to stand beyond time, beyond life itself. How to look at them, what to think, what to say – was more than his human brain could

41

grasp. The simplest, everyday things – taking them by the hand, kissing them, saying, 'Hello, Dad . . .' – seemed unbelievably horrible because of the monstrous inhumanity, craziness and falsity of it all.

After being sentenced, the condemned prisoners were not sent together to one cell as Kovalchuk had assumed, but were returned to solitary confinement, and all morning, right up to eleven o'clock, when his parents arrived, Sergey Golovin walked furiously up and down his cell, plucking at his little beard, scowling pathetically and muttering to himself. Now and then he would stop in mid-stride, take in a chestful of air and blow it back out like someone who has been too long underwater. But he was so fit, so full of life and youth, that even in these moments of the utmost cruelty and suffering the blood surged strongly under his skin, giving his cheeks a rosy glow, and his blue eyes were radiant with innocence.

However, things turned out much better than expected for Sergey.

First into the meeting room was Nikolay Sergeyevich Golovin, a retired colonel. He was white all over – face, beard, hair and hands – like a marble statue in men's clothing, and he was wearing the same old short coat, showing its age a bit but nicely cleaned, smelling of benzine and sporting some nice new transverse epaulettes. He marched in decisively with the firm tread of a military man, extended a dry white hand and spoke in a loud voice. 'Hello, Sergey.'

He was followed by Sergey's mother, mincing in with an awkward smile on her face. But she too shook hands and spoke in a loud voice. 'Hello, darling.'

She kissed him on the lips and sat down without saying anything more. She had not rushed in, cried out or made any kind of scene, as Sergey had feared. She had simply kissed him and sat down. And she had even begun to straighten her black silk dress with trembling hands.

What Sergey did not know was that all the previous night the colonel had locked himself away in his small study, summoned all his strength and worked on this ritual occasion. 'We must lighten our son's burden, not add to it in his last minutes' was the colonel's firm conclusion, and he carefully weighed every possible phrase, every gesture, that might come into tomorrow's conversation. But he kept losing his way, forgetting the few bits he had managed to prepare, and he wept bitter tears as he sat there tucked into a corner of the oilcloth divan. And in the morning he outlined for his wife's benefit how they were to conduct themselves at the meeting.

'The main thing is – kiss and keep quiet,' was his instruction. 'You can say something a bit later on, but when you kiss him you mustn't say anything. Don't speak when you've just kissed him. Do you understand? If you do, it will come out all wrong.'

'Yes, Nikolay.'

'And don't cry. For God's sake, don't start crying. You'll be the death of him if you do, woman!'

'Why are you crying then?'

'You'd bring anybody to tears. But you mustn't cry. Do you hear what I say?'

'All right, Nikolay.'

He had intended to run through his instructions once again in the cab, but he forgot. So there they had been, driving along in silence, two bent figures, grey and old both of them, lost in thought, while the city was enjoying itself in noisy celebrations. It was Shrovetide and everyone was out on the noisy streets.

Now, they had sat down. The colonel assumed his well-rehearsed attitude, with his right hand tucked under his coat lapel. Sergey had been sitting down for no more than a moment when he caught sight of his mother's wrinkled face close to and leapt up.

'Don't get up, Seryozha, darling,' his mother implored.

'Sit down, Sergey,' said his father.

None of them spoke. His mother still had an awkward smile on her face. 'We did what we could to help you, Seryozha, darling.'

'Didn't do any good, Mamma . . .'

The colonel's response was firm. 'We had to do it, Sergey, so you wouldn't think your parents had abandoned you.'

There was another short silence. They were too scared to pronounce any word; it was as if every word on their tongues lost its meaning, and there was only one meaning: death. Sergey took a look at his father's nicely cleaned coat, still smelling of benzine, and thought. 'There's no servant now, so he must have cleaned it himself. Why did I never notice him cleaning that coat before? Must have done it early morning.' Then suddenly he asked a question. 'How's my sister getting on? Is she all right?'

'Ninochka doesn't know.' His mother was quick to respond.

But the colonel cut in sharply. 'What's the point in lying about it? She read about it in the papers, poor girl. Let

Sergey know that we all . . . his nearest and dearest . . . at the right time . . . were thinking about . . .'

He stopped, unable to carry on. Suddenly his wife's face crumpled all at once, swimming with tears, convulsing, wild and wet. Her lacklustre eyes darted around crazily; her breathing became more hurried, rushed and noisy.

'Se— Ser— Se— Se—' she kept on repeating without moving her lips. 'Se—'

'Mamma!'

The colonel took a step forward and, shaking all over in every fold of his coat and every line on his face, unaware of how terrifying he looked in his deathly whiteness and desperately agonizing determination, spoke to his wife. 'Stop that! Stop tormenting him! Don't! Don't torment him! He's going to die! Don't torment him!'

She had been intimidated into silence, but he was still shaking his clenched fists in front of his chest, striving for self-control. 'Don't torment him!'

Then he stepped back, tucked a trembling hand under his coat lapel, and with an expression of grimly forced calm, he asked a question, white-lipped. 'When?'

'Tomorrow morning,' replied Sergey, equally white-lipped.

His mother looked down, her lips champing; she seemed not to be taking anything in.

Still champing, she seemed to be pouring out words that were primitive and unnatural. 'Ninochka sends you a kiss, Seryozhenka.'

'Send one back from me,' said Sergey.

'Right. And the Khvostovs want to be remembered to you.'

'Who? Oh, yes, the Khvostovs.'

The colonel cut across them. 'Well, we'd better be off. On your feet, Mother. It's time.'

The two of them assisted the sagging woman to her feet.

'Say goodbye,' ordered the colonel. 'Sign of the Cross.'

She did what she was told. But as she crossed herself and gave her son the lightest of kisses, she shook her head and her speech became incoherent. 'No, not like that. No, no. Not like that. No, no. Me . . . after . . . What can I say? No, not like that.'

'Goodbye, Sergey,' said his father.

They shook hands, and held each other in a close but short-lived embrace.

'You . . .' began Sergey.

'What?' snapped his father.

'No, not like that. No, no. Not like that. What can I say?' His mother was still rambling and shaking her head. She had managed to get herself seated again, and she was shaking all over.

'You . . .' Sergey began again.

Suddenly his face was that of a pitiful child; it crumpled, and his eyes flooded with tears. Through their sparkling mist he could see his father's white face close to, with tears like his own.

'You're a noble man, Father.'

'What? What *are* you saying?' said the colonel, horrified.

And suddenly, like a broken man, he let his head fall across his son's shoulder. He had once been taller than Sergey, but now he had shrunk down to a smaller height, and his dry, fluffy head lay like a little white ball on his son's shoulder. And they were both silently but warmly embracing; Sergey kissed the fluffy white hair, his father the prison smock.

'What about *me*?' came a sudden loud voice.

They turned to look. Sergey's mother was standing there with her head thrown back, watching in fury, almost hatred.

'What is it, Mother?' cried the colonel.

'What about *me*?' she said, shaking her head, with the intensity of a demented mind. 'You can kiss goodbye, but what about *me*? It's all right for you *men*. But *what about me*? Eh?'

'Mamma, darling!' Sergey threw himself at her.

What followed cannot and need not be conveyed.

The colonel's last words were: 'I give you my blessing as you go to your death, Seryozha. Die with courage, an officer's death.'

Then they left. Left, but didn't leave. They stayed on, stood around, spoke – then they were gone. Mamma had been sitting there, Papa had been there, standing, and suddenly, somehow, they were gone. Back in his cell, Sergey lay down on his bunk, turned to face the wall to shield himself from the guards, and wept and wept. Then, weary from weeping, he fell into a deep sleep.

Only one person, his mother, came to see Vassily Kashirin; his father hadn't wanted to come. When his mother arrived, Vassily was pacing up and down his room, shivering with cold even though it was a warm day, almost hot. Their conversation was brief and grim.

'You shouldn't have come, Mamma darling. It's an ordeal for you and for me.'

'Why, Vasya? Why did you do it? God in heaven!'

The old woman broke down in tears, wiping them away with the fringe of black wool on her scarf.

Doing what he and his brothers always did, he bawled at his mother, who was completely at a loss, and then suddenly stopped, shivering with cold, and snapped at her angrily. 'Look at this! I knew it! Mamma, you just don't understand – anything at all!'

'All right. All right. What's wrong with you? Are you cold?'

'Yes,' he said, cutting in, and off he went pacing around the room, scowling angrily at her in sideways glances.

'Happen you've caught cold?'

'Mamma, it's got nothing to do with catching cold. It's . . .' And he gave up on her with a wave of despair.

The old woman was intending to say, 'And our old man wants pancakes on Monday,' but she lost her nerve and wailed at him. 'It's our son, I said. You must come . . . Forgive him his sins . . . Old goat wouldn't listen . . .'

'To hell with him. He's no father of mine. Been a swine all his life, and he still is!'

'Vasya, darling, he *is* your father!' The old woman recoiled in disapproval.

'My father, huh!'

'Your own father!'

'Oh yes?'

It was all frantic and absurd. Death lay ahead, yet this trivial, unnecessary, futile bit of nonsense was building up, and their words were crunching like empty nutshells underfoot. Almost in tears – tears of anguish caused by the perpetual failure to communicate that had walled him off throughout his life from friends and family and even now, in the hour of his death itself, stared him in the face with all its meanness and stupidity – Vassily cried out. 'Can't you see they're going to hang me? *Hang* me. Can you see it, yes or no? Hang me!'

'Well, if you hadn't done things to people, maybe they wouldn't . . .'

'For the love of God! What are you on about? Wild animals don't behave like this. Am I your son, or *not*?'

He burst into tears and sat down in one corner. The old lady wept too, in her own corner. Incapable of joining for a single minute in a bond of love and setting that against the horror of impending death, they wept cold tears of solitude that brought no warmth to the heart.

His mother spoke. 'You're asking me whether I'm a mother or not. You're blaming me. But these last few days I've gone grey with worry. I'm an old woman now. And you keep on blaming me.'

'All right, Mamma. It's all right. I'm sorry. It's time you went. Kiss my brothers for me.'

'Am I really not a mother to you? Don't I show any pity?'

Then at last she was gone. She had walked away weeping bitterly, wiping her eyes on the fringes of her scarf, and not seeing where she was going. And the further she got from the prison, the more she wept her scalding tears. She turned around and walked back towards the prison, only to get completely lost in the town where she had been born, raised and lived through to old age. She fetched up in a kind of run-down patch of garden under a few old trees with snapped-off branches, where she sat down on a bench wet from the thaw. And suddenly it came to her: they were going to hang him tomorrow.

The old woman leapt to her feet with every intention of running away, but suddenly her head spun violently and she collapsed. The little path was slippery, swimming with ice and, try as she might, she couldn't get to her feet. She kept on spinning round, and when she tried to raise herself on her elbows and knees, she slipped back down on her side. The black scarf slithered off her head, exposing a bald patch among the dirty-grey hair at the back. For some reason she felt as if she was at a wedding, enjoying the celebrations – her son was getting married. She had had more than a glass or two of wine and was getting very drunk.

'No more,' she cried, turning it away. 'For the love of God, I can't take any more.' Her head was reeling as she slithered over the thin crust of ice covering the snow, but still it came – more and more wine, poured out for her.

And her heart began to ache from the drunken laughter, the rich spread of food and the crazy dancing – but they went on pouring out more wine for her. More and more wine.

6. THE HOURS FLY BY

In the fortress where the condemned terrorists were imprisoned, there was a bell-tower with an ancient clock. Every hour, every half-hour, every quarter of an hour, a chime rang out in a long, slow toll, a sound of sadness high overhead that gradually ebbed away, like the distant, plaintive call of passing birds. During the day this strange sad music was lost in the sounds of the wide and bustling city street that ran past the fortress. Trams rattled up and down, horses clip-clopped, automobiles bounced and swooped, announcing their presence well in advance. It was Shrovetide, and some peasant drivers had come in specially from the city outskirts in carnival mood, and the little bells strung around the necks of their diminutive horses filled the air with a steady jingle. And there was a murmur of speaking voices, the slightly intoxicated and cheery tones of people on holiday. The discordant bustle was in tune with the early spring thaw with its dirty puddles on the pavements and the trees all around the square that had gone black overnight. A warm breeze wafted in from the sea in wide, wet flurries. It was almost as if the watching eye could observe tiny particles of fresh air being borne away in a cloud of goodwill, off into the freedom of infinite distance, laughing as they went.

At night the street lapsed into repose under the lonely glow of large electric suns. Now the huge fortress, its flat walls showing no spark of light, withdrew steadily into darkness and quietude, cutting itself off beyond a cordon of silence and stillness from the living and ever-active city. At this time the chiming asserted itself again, its weird, unearthly tune slowly and sadly proceeding overhead from birth to death. It was born and reborn, its false message for the ears ringing out in soft and sombre tones and a dying fall, only to ring out anew. It was like big, limpid droplets of glass tinkling out a muted chime as they fell from ineffable heights into a metal bowl filled with hours and minutes. Or like birds of passage flying by.

By day and by night this chime was the only sound to penetrate the separate cells where the condemned criminals were held in solitary confinement. It came in through the roof and through the thick stone walls, shivering the silence, and it went away imperceptibly, only to return no less imperceptibly. Sometimes they didn't hear it, and forgot about it; sometimes they waited for it in despair, living from chime to chime, no longer trusting the silence. Only the most serious criminals were assigned to this prison, which lived by its own rules – strict, harsh rules, as rough as a corner wall of the fortress itself – and if there could be nobility in a ruthless regime, it was the nobility of dead silence, hollow and soundlessly solemn, picking up whispers and the slightest breath.

And amidst this solemn silence, disrupted only by a lugubrious chime marking the fleeting minutes, five people – two women and three men – cut off from every living thing, awaited the onset of night, dawn and execution, each preparing for it in his or her own way.

7. THERE IS NO DEATH

Tanya Kovalchuk behaved as she had done throughout her whole life in thinking only of other people and never about herself; here and now, suffering only on behalf of the others, she was most upset. She could imagine imminent death presenting itself as an agonizing reality for Seryozha Golovin, for Musya and the rest of them, but it did not seem to concern her at all.

And, as if to reward herself for her own much-needed self-control in court, she now wept for hours on end, in the way you would expect from old women who have known much sorrow, or young ones full of compassion, people of exceptional kindness. And the idea that Seryozha might not get his tobacco, or Werner might be deprived of his strong tea, together with the thought of them all inevitably dying, seemed to cause her more anguish than the idea of execution itself. Execution is something inexorable, even incidental, not worth thinking about, but for a man in prison, waiting for execution, the loss of his tobacco is intolerable. She started to reminisce, running through lovely details of their lives together, and she died a thousand deaths, terrified by the idea of Seryozha meeting his parents.

It was for Musya that she felt sorriest of all. For some time now she had been under the impression that Musya was in love with Werner, and although there was no truth in this, Tanya had persisted in dreaming up something nice and bright for the two of them. When they were still free, Musya had worn a little silver ring decorated with a skull and cross-bones within a crown of thorns. Tanya Kovalchuk had often looked at this ring with an aching heart, seeing it as a symbol of doom, and she had begged Musya, half jokingly, half seriously, to take it off.

'Give it to me,' she had begged.

'No, Tanya, I'm not doing that. You'll soon have a different kind of ring on your finger.'

For some reason the others in their turn had assumed she was bound to get married very soon, and this annoyed her because she had no desire for a husband. And so, as she recalled that half-humorous banter with Musya, and the fact that she was now definitely doomed, she found herself choking on tears of motherly compassion. And every time the clock chimed, she looked up with a tear-stained face and listened to it, wondering how the others were reacting in their cells to the steadily insistent summons of death.

But Musya herself felt happy.

With her hands behind her back, tucked into the ill-fitting prison smock that made her look rather odd, like a man or a young lad dressed in someone else's clothes, she paced the floor, up and down, tirelessly. The sleeves of the smock were too long for her, and she had rolled them up, with her thin, scrawny arms, almost those of a child, poking out from gaping holes like the stalks of flowers sticking out of a cheap and dirty old pot. The rough material had been rubbing and chafing her delicate white neck, and from time to time she would reach up with both hands to free her throat and finger the sore places on her livid skin.

Musya paced the floor, to and fro, her features flushing with the effort of vindicating herself in the eyes of the world. She wanted vindication because she was only a slip of a girl with nothing special about her, nothing heroic, not much in the way of achievement, and yet she was going to be subjected to the same kind of gloriously honourable death visited upon true heroes and martyrs before her time. With her unshakeable faith in human kindness, compassion and love, she could imagine people worrying about her at this moment, suffering with pain and pity, and the shame of it flooded her face red. It was as if she was doing something thoroughly disgraceful by going to the scaffold.

At the last meeting with the defence lawyer, she had asked him to get some poison for her, but she had thought better of it: what might he and the others think – that she was showing off or chickening out, and instead of dying a quiet, inconspicuous death she was making a song and dance about it? So she added hastily, 'No, no, don't bother.'

Now there was only one thing she wanted: to make people understand that she was not being at all heroic, that dying isn't all that terrible and people shouldn't feel sorry or worry about her. To let them see that it wasn't her fault they were making such a meal of putting her to death like that when she was so young and insignificant.

Like someone charged with a real offence, Musya was looking for exoneration, for anything at all that would enhance her sacrifice and give it real value. This was her line of thinking: 'Yes, I'm still young and I might have lived a long life, but still . . .'

It was like a candle fading in the bright light of the rising sun: her young age and life itself came out dark and dismal against the glorious radiance about to shine upon her modest head. There was no exoneration.

But what about that special spirit within her – limitless love, limitless readiness to take on big things, an unlimited capacity for selflessness? It really wasn't her fault she had not been given the opportunity to do everything she had wanted and intended to do – that she had been killed on the temple threshold, at the foot of the sacrificial altar.

55

But if that's how things go, if a person is to be judged not by what he has done, but by what he intended to do, well then . . . then she was worthy of a martyr's crown.

'Am I?' thought Musya sheepishly. 'Am I really worthy of that? Worthy enough for people to weep and grieve over me when I am so small and insignificant?'

And a feeling of indescribable joy came over her. There was no doubt about it, not a moment's hesitation; she had been taken to their bosom, she had every right to stand alongside those noble souls who from time immemorial had attained the highest heaven by going to the stake, suffering under torture and submitting to execution. This was peace, resplendent and restful, a gentle glow of infinite happiness. It was as if she had already gone from the earth, soaring bodiless into the sunshine realm of truth and life.

'So that's death, is it? How can you call it death?' thought Musya in her blissful state.

And if all the world's scientists, philosophers and executioners had come together in her cell and laid before her their books, scalpels, axes and nooses to demonstrate that death exists, that man dies and gets killed, and that there is no immortality – she would have been bemused. What do you mean there is no immortality, when here she is, now, immortal? What price immortality, what price death, when, here and now, she is already dead and already immortal, as alive in death as she has been alive in life?

And if they had carried a foul-stinking coffin into her cell, containing her own decomposing body, and said, 'Look, that's you,' she would have taken one glance and told them, 'No, that's not me.'

And if they had tried to show her the menacing sight of decomposition, and scare into believing it was her – *really her!* – Musya would have responded with a smile, and said, 'No. You *think* that is me, but it isn't. I'm the person you are talking to. How could I be *that*?'

'No, but you are going to die, and *that's* what you'll become.'

'No. I'm not going to die.'

'You're going to be executed. Look, there's the noose.'

'I'm going to be executed, but I shan't die. How can I die when I'm already immortal, here and now?'

And the scientists, philosophers and executioners would step back, and say in quavering tones, 'Do not touch this place. It is holy ground.'

What did Musya have in mind? Many things – for her the thread of life, far from being broken by death, would go on spinning out smoothly and evenly. She thought of her comrades, both the faraway people who would be painfully hurt by their execution and those close to her who would mount the same scaffold. She was taken aback by Vassily's terrible fear – he had always been so brave, even enjoying a joke with death. Take that Tuesday morning when they were tying the explosives onto their belts which would blow them to pieces in a few hours' time. Tanya Kovalchuk's hands were shaking so much from anxiety that she had to be taken away, but Vassily was in a jokey mood, clowning about and spinning round without a care in the world, and Werner had to take him to task: 'Don't mess about with death.'

So what was he now so afraid of?

But this incomprehensible fear was so alien to Musya's spirit that she soon stopped worrying about him and trying to fathom its cause. Suddenly she felt a sharp urge to see Seryozha Golovin and have a laugh with him. After a few moments' thought, she felt an even more desperate urge to see Werner and chew the fat with him. And, imagining that Werner was walking alongside her with his measured stride and his heels digging into the ground, Musya spoke to him. 'No, Werner, my dear, that's nonsense. It doesn't matter whether you killed N.N. or not. You're a clever man, but this is like one of your games of chess. You take one piece, then another, and eventually you win. The only thing that matters is that you and I are ready to die. Can't you see that? Those gentlemen, what do they think? That there's nothing more horrible than death? They have invented death, they're scared of it, and they want us to be scared. I'll tell you what I'd like to do – walk out on my own with a Browning in front of a whole regiment and shoot at them all. As long as there are thousands of them and I am alone, I won't kill anybody. That's the only thing – there must be thousands of them. When thousands kill one person, that person is the one who wins. That's how it is, Werner, my dear.'

But this was so clear she felt there was no point in arguing any further. Werner must have seen it himself by now. Or maybe her thoughts simply didn't want to settle in one place – they were like a blithely cruising bird with a view of limitless horizons, and a grasp of infinite space, ultimate depths and the serenity of blue skies, tender and caressing. The clock chimed incessantly, shocking the deadly silence, and her thoughts blended with the lovely harmony of that distant sound, which set them ringing too and turned all her fluid and fleeting impressions into music. For Musya, it was like going for a carriage-drive in the tender darkness of the night, down a smooth, wide highway, with the springs rocking gently and the little bells tinkling. All her cares and worries had gone, her weary body had melted away in the darkness, and her serenely sleepy mind formed the brightest of silent images for her to wallow in, revelling in their colours and the perfect rest that came with them. Musya brought to mind her three colleagues, recently hanged; their bright and joyful faces seemed so close to her – closer than anyone still living. She felt like a man looking forward happily in the morning to walking in that evening and greeting old friends at home with a smile upon his lips.

Musya felt very tired from so much walking. She lay down cautiously on the bunk, and carried on daydreaming with her eyes lightly closed. The clock chimed incessantly, shocking the unbroken silence, and bright images floated softly within its singing bounds. Musya was thinking: 'Is this really death? Heavens, how beautiful it is! Or is it life? I don't know. I really don't know. I shall go on watching and listening.'

For some time now, ever since the first days of incarceration, her hearing had been playing tricks with her. Well attuned to music, it had been whetted by the silence, against which it turned tiny particles of reality – guards walking down the corridor, the chiming of the clock, the wind rustling over the iron roof, a creaking lantern – into musical patterns. To begin with, Musya was afraid of them, and she chased them away like morbid hallucinations, but then she saw that she was fine and there was nothing at all morbid about them. She began to relax and give in to them. And now, suddenly, she could definitely make out the clear strains of military music. She opened her eyes in astonishment and looked up. It was night outside, and the clock was chiming. That's it again, she thought calmly, and closed her eyes. The moment they were closed, the music came again – clearly audible music from around the corner, with soldiers, a whole regiment, marching up the right-hand side and going past her window. Their feet were beating out the time on the frozen ground – left, right, left, right – and you could even hear the creaking of a leather boot now and then, or a foot slipping somewhere and then picking up its stride. Nearer and nearer came the music, something completely unfamiliar – but a loud and cheery festival march. Some celebration was clearly underway in the fortress.

Now the band was outside her window, and the whole cell was filled with happy sounds and cheerful harmonies in different registers. One big brass instrument was painfully out, lagging behind the beat one minute, then ridiculously galloping ahead. Musya could see the diminutive soldier playing this instrument, and the effort on his face made her laugh.

They're going now. Their steps trail away – left, right, left, right. From far away the music sounds even better, jollier. One or two departing false notes from the cheerily booming brass, and they've gone. And now the clock chimes again from the bell-tower, with its slow, sad tones barely troubling the stillness.

'They've gone,' thought Musya with a touch of regret. She

misses the cheery, funny sounds, now they are lost. She even misses the lost soldiers, because those men with their squeaky boots, struggling so hard with their brass instruments, are not the same people, they are a completely different lot from the ones she wanted to shoot at with her Browning.

'Please come back,' she begged plaintively. And back they came. Here they are, bending over her, enveloping her in a limpid cloud, raising her up to where birds of passage soar on high, calling out like town criers. They swoop right and left, up and down, calling out like town-criers. They voice their cries, their proclamations, announcing their flight from afar. They spread their wings wide open, the darkness bears them up like the daylight, and the swell of their breasts, scything the air, radiates a blue reflection of the resplendent city below. Her heartbeat slows to a steady pace; her breathing is now gentle and easy. She is falling asleep. Her face is weary and pale, there are circles under her eyes, and her young girl's arms look skinny and emaciated. There is a smile on her lips. Tomorrow at sunrise this human face will be contorted into an inhuman grimace, the brain will be clogged with thickened blood and glassy eyes will bulge from their sockets – but today she sleeps in peace, smiling in her splendid immortality.

Musya is asleep.

And prison-life goes on, a life of deafness and hearing, of blindness and sight, a kind of unending angst. Someone, somewhere, is walking about. Someone, somewhere, is whispering. Somewhere, someone rattles a gun. Was that a scream? Maybe not – just a noise in the stillness.

The peephole in the door opens noiselessly. A dark, whisk-ered face appears in the dark aperture, stares in at Musya, watching her for some time in amazement, and disappears as softly as it came.

The chimes ring out with agonizing slowness, as if the weary hours are climbing the steep slope to midnight, and the upward movement gets heavier and harder. Then they slip and slide back down, moaning, only to crawl up again, agonizingly, towards their black summit.

Someone, somewhere, is walking about. Someone, some-where, is whispering. And now horses are being harnessed to black carriages which carry no lights.

8. DEATH EXISTS. SO DOES LIFE

Sergey Golovin had given no thought to death, which had seemed so irrelevant, of no concern to him. He was a fit, strong and buoyant young man, endowed with a happy-go-lucky attitude and sheer *joie de vivre* that allowed him to cope with any unpleasant or life-threatening thoughts and feelings by absorbing them into his system quickly and without trace. In the same way that his cuts, wounds and grazes soon healed up, anything painful, wounding his spirit, worked its way out of him and gradually disappeared. And to everything, business or pleasure – photography, cycling or planning terrorism – he brought the same easy-going and life-affirming sense of application. Everything in life was good fun, everything in life was important, every-thing must be done well.

And everything he did was done well; he could manage a sail marvellously, he was very good with a pistol, devoted in friendship and in love, and he had a fanatical belief in one's 'word of honour'. His friends laughed at him; they said that if a police agent, a snout, a notorious spy, swore on his 'word of honour' that he wasn't a spy, Sergey would believe him and shake him by the hand like a friend. If he had a fault, it was only that he fancied himself as a singer, when he had no ear for music: his singing was appalling. He couldn't hold a tune, even in songs of revolution, and he wasn't best pleased when they laughed at him.

'You're all stupid asses. Either that, or I'm one,' he would say to them, looking serious and obviously offended. People would match his serious manner, but they were of one accord, and they came to the same considered opinion: 'You're the ass. You sound like one.'

Yet for this fault of character – as often happens with nice people – he was loved perhaps as much as he was for his virtues.

He was so unafraid of death, so uninterested in it, that before they left Tanya Kovalchuk's flat on the fateful morning, he was the only one who had a good breakfast, putting away two glasses of tea, half full of milk, and a decent-sized roll. Then he looked ruefully at Werner's untouched roll, and said, 'Why don't you eat something? You should. You need building up.'

'Don't feel like it.'

'You're a good trencherman, Seryozha.'

Instead of replying, Sergey burst into song, with his mouth still full. His singing was raucous and tuneless: '*Dark whirling winds swirl overhead . . .*'

After his arrest, he could have been depressed: it had not been done well, they had failed, but now he thought, 'Here's something else that must be done well. We have to die well,' and this cheered him up. And, strange to relate, from the second morning in the fortress, he had started doing exercises prescribed in an extraordinary 'rationalized' programme created by some German by the name of Müller, which had caught his imagination. He would strip naked and, to the amazement and alarm of the watching sentry, he would work his way steadily through all eighteen set exercises. The fact that there was a sentry observing this with obvious surprise, delighted him, as a disciple of the Müller method, and, although he knew there would be no response, he would talk to the eye that was peering in through the little window.

'Don't worry, my friend. It's building me up. You could do with this in your regiment,' he would call out persuasively, keeping it short to avoid frightening anyone, without ever suspecting that the soldier simply thought he was mad.

The fear of death started to come over him bit by bit, in a kind of series of sudden shocks. It was like an uppercut, a fist smashing up into his heart, hard. More like a sharp pain than fear. Then the sensation would be forgotten, only for it to return a few hours later, lasting longer and hurting more every time it came. And it was clearly beginning to take on the rough outline of a ghastly, unbearable terror.

'What – me scared?' thought Sergey. 'Stupid idea!'

It wasn't him being scared, it was his young body, fit and strong, which he had been unable to fool despite the German's physical exercises or any amount of rubbing down with a cold, wet towel. And as it gained strength and freshness from the application of cold water, it suffered all the more unbearably from fleeting shocks of dread. And it was during the very moments when he experienced a lift of the spirit from sheer *joie de vivre* and bodily strength, in the morning, after a good night's sleep and a stiff work-out, that he felt a sharp stab of terror that seemed to come from outside. He took note of this, and thought to himself: 'Don't be stupid, brother Sergey. To make death easier you have to weaken the body, not build it up. Don't be so stupid!'

And he stopped doing the exercises and towelling down. For the benefit of the soldier, he shouted out, by way of explanation and justification: 'I'm packing it in, but don't get me wrong, brother. It is the right thing to do. It's no good for anybody who's going to get hanged. It's still all right for everybody else.'

And it really did seem to make a difference. He also tried eating less to make himself feel weaker, but despite the lack of fresh air and exercise, he couldn't stop feeling hungry. This was difficult to deal with, and he gobbled up everything they put before him. Then he tried something different: before starting his meal he would scrape half the hot food off into a pail. It seemed to help. He began to feel weary and drowsy.

'I'll show you what's what!' he warned his body, gently running saddened fingers over his feeble, run-down muscles.

But it wasn't long before his body got used to this new regime, and the dread of death came back. Admittedly the pain wasn't quite as fierce or fiery, but it nagged at him and made him feel sick. 'It's because of all the waiting,' thought Sergey. 'Best thing would be to sleep right through to the hanging.' And he tried that, trying to sleep as long as he could. At first it worked, but soon, either because he had slept too much or for some other reason, he began suffering from insomnia. And along with that came clear, sharp thinking and a longing for life.

'What – me scared? To hell with that for an idea.' He was obsessed with death. 'It's such a pity about life. It's a wonderful thing, whatever the pessimists say about it. What happens when they hang a pessimist? *He* thinks it's a pity about life. A real pity. And what's this – why has my beard grown? For ages and ages it wouldn't grow at all, and now it has. What for?'

And he would shake his head at the sadness of it all, heaving his heart out in great, long sighs. Silence – then a deep, long sigh. More silence – and another sigh, longer and heavier.

That was how things stood right up to the trial and that last ghastly encounter with the old men. He woke up in his cell acutely aware that everything to do with living was over, and that ahead lay nothing but a few hours of waiting in emptiness, and then death – and it all seemed very strange. He felt as if he had been completely stripped in a most unusual way – stripped not only of his clothes, but also robbed of the sun, the air, sound and light, action and speech. As yet there was no death, but life had gone, already replaced by something new, something impenetrably obscure, either without any meaning or possessed of a meaning that was so profound, so mysterious and inhuman, that it could never be grasped.

'Hell's teeth!' said Sergey in anguished amazement. 'What *is* all this? Where do *I* come into it? What's left of *me*?'

He took stock of himself closely, all over, fascinated by what he saw, from the baggy prison slippers to his own belly sticking out from his prison smock. He walked around his cell with his arms stretched out, still absorbed in himself like a woman trying on a new dress which is too long for her. He willed his head to turn, and it did turn. And this . . . this thing that somehow seemed rather frightening . . . this was *him*, Sergey Golovin, and this is what would cease to be.

And everything had become unreal.

He tried walking around his cell – and walking seemed unreal. He tried sitting down – and sitting seemed unreal. He tried taking a drink of water – and it seemed unreal that he was drinking, swallowing, holding a mug, using fingers, trembling fingers. He choked on the water, and as he cleared his throat and gave a cough, he thought to himself, 'I'm coughing. It's not real.'

'Am I going round the bend, damn it?' thought Sergey with a chilly feeling. 'Bloody hell, that's all I need!'

He rubbed his forehead with one hand, and even that seemed unreal. Then, holding his breath, he froze and stayed motionless for what seemed hours on end, extinguishing all thought, suppressing his deep breathing and avoiding any kind of movement – because the slightest thought meant madness, the slightest movement meant madness. Time had gone, it seemed to have been converted into space – translucent and airless – a vast physical area with everything there upon it, the earth, life and people, and all of it could be absorbed at a single glance, all of it right up to the end, to the very edge of mystery, to death itself. Some sacrilegious hand had drawn aside the age-old curtain hiding the mystery of life and the mystery of death, rendering them no longer mysterious, though still incomprehensible. It was like a truth engraved in a foreign language. His human brain had no access to the concepts, and his human speech had no access to the words, needed to capture what he had seen. And if the words 'I'm dead scared' had any meaning, it was only because there were no other words available, no other concepts that corresponded to this new, inhuman condition – their existence was impossible. It would be like this if a human being, with only his human capacity for understanding, his experience and his feelings to go on, were suddenly to get a glimpse of God himself, seeing without understanding, even though he knew this thing was called God. He would be left shuddering with the unimaginable agony of unimaginable incomprehension.

'That's what Müller does for you!' he shouted out loud with incredible passion, shaking his head. And with that sudden change of feeling that the human spirit is so prone to, he laughed with genuine delight. 'Oh Müller! My dear old Müller! My truly wonderful German friend! But you are quite right, brother Müller. I'm the ass here.'

He walked around his cell a few times and then amazed the soldier observing him through the peephole by stripping himself naked and applying himself diligently to a performance of all eighteen exercises. He stretched his young, rather slimmed-down body upwards and outwards, squatted on his heels and strained up on tiptoes, inhaling and exhaling, flinging his arms and legs out wide. And after each exercise he spoke out smugly. 'That's the way to do it! That's the real thing, brother Müller!'

His cheeks glowed, and droplets of lovely, hot sweat emerged from every pore; his heartbeat was steady and strong.

'The thing is, Müller,' thought Sergey, expanding his chest so that his ribs were clearly outlined under the taut, thin skin. 'The thing is this. There is a nineteenth exercise: hanging by the neck from a fixed position. It's called execution. Do you get that, Müller? They take a living being – say Sergey Golovin – they wrap him up like a doll, and hang him by the neck until he is dead. It's a stupid thing to do, Müller, but it can't be helped. It's got to happen.'

He turned over onto his right side, and repeated himself: 'It's got to happen, brother Müller.'

9. HORROR IN SOLITARY

To the same chimes, only a few empty cells along from Sergey and Musya, though as desperately lonely as if he was the only living creature in the universe, the miserable Vassily

Kashirin was ending his life in anguish and terror. Covered in sweat, with his wet shirt clinging to his body and his once curly hair all over the place, he rushed around his cell frantic with despair like a man with unbearable toothache. He would sit down for a while, then get up and run or press his forehead against the wall or search for something with his eyes, as if he was looking for medicine. He had changed so much that he seemed to have had two different faces: his earlier face, a young one, had gone away to be replaced by a new one, a terrible face emerging from darkness.

He had been suddenly overwhelmed by a fear of death, which had seized him completely and now held him in its grip. Only that morning, while staring death in the face, he had been 'messing about' with it, but by evening, in the solitary confinement of his cell, he had been engulfed and flattened by an inexorable tide of terror. While he had always been risking danger and death on his own terms, and had kept control over his own death, however terrible it might be, he had carried on flippantly, even enjoying himself. Any suggestion of a wrinkled, old-womanish fear was submerged in a spirit of absolute freedom and the need to prove his daring and fearless character through sheer strength of will. Fastening the belt which carried the infernal machine, he seemed to *become* the infernal machine, assuming the ruthless reasoning of dynamite as he acquired its fire-power and death-dealing energy. And as he made his way along the street through the busy throng of people absorbed in their own workaday concerns, skipping out of the way of cab-horses and trams, he felt like a new arrival from an unknown alien realm where there was no knowledge of death or fear.

Then suddenly – a sharp, savage, shattering change. He was no longer going where *he* wanted to go; he was being taken where other people wanted him to go. He could no longer choose a place to be; they were putting him into a stone cage and locking him up like an inanimate object. He was no longer free to make his own decisions about living or dying like everybody else; they were definitely and inevitably going to put him to death. In a split-second he, the incarnation of strong will, life and strength, had come to be a pathetic example of helplessness unique in all the world, newly transformed into an animal lined up for slaughter, an empty thing incapable of speech that could be moved around, set fire to, broken up. Not a word of anything he said would ever be heard, and if he started screaming they would gag him. If he moved his legs, they would take him away and hang him, and if he showed any resistance, put up a struggle or lay down on the ground, they would force him to his feet, tie him up and take him away, bound hand and foot to the gallows. And the fact that the mechanical procedure being thrust upon him was being carried out by people just like him made them seem weird, unreal and sinister, either phantoms, creatures of pretence intent on deception, or mechanized marionettes worked by springs: designed to fetch and grab, take away, hang, pull down on his legs. To cut through rope, haul down, cart away and bury. And from the very first day of his imprisonment, people and life became for him an unbelievably horrific world consisting of these phantoms and mechanized marionettes.

All but speechless from terror, he tried to convince himself that they did have tongues and the power of speech, but he couldn't bring himself to believe it: they seemed unable to talk. He tried to remember them speaking and what their words had meant when they were in communication, but he couldn't. Their mouths gaped open, sounds came out, they walked around, and that's all they did.

This is what you would feel like if, one night when you were at home alone, all the pieces of furniture came to life, moved about and took complete control of you. Suddenly they would have you up before the court – cupboard, chair, desk and sofa. You could remonstrate and chase around, begging for mercy and screaming for help, but they would rabbit on with each other in their own language, and then dispatch you to be hanged – that cupboard, chair, desk and sofa. With the other household objects looking on.

And Vassily Kashirin, sentenced to be hanged by the neck until dead, began to see the whole thing as Toyland: his cell, the door with its peephole, the chiming of the well-wound clock, the intricately sculpted fortress building, and especially that mechanized marionette with a gun, stamping up and down the corridor, and all the others who stared at him scarily through the little window, and brought him food without talking. And what he was experiencing was not the fear of death – no, if anything he wanted to die. Death, in all its age-old, unfathomable mystery, was more susceptible to reason than this world, which had turned into something so savage and fantastic. Besides, death was somehow being steadily and completely extinguished in a crazy world of phantoms and puppets, and losing its enormous and mysterious significance as it also became a mechanical process and only for that reason something to be dreaded. Fetch and grab, take away, hang, pull down on the legs. Cut rope, haul down, cart away and bury.

A man has gone from the world.

In court, a spirit of comradeship had brought Kashirin to his senses, and just for a moment he had been able to see people again. They were sitting there, trying him and saying things to each other in human speech; they were also listening, and seemed to be taking things in. But at the meeting with his mother, with the horror of a man who is losing his reason and knows it, he had clearly sensed that this old woman in a black headscarf was nothing more than a cleverly constructed mechanical doll – one of those that can say 'Da-da' or 'Ma-mma', only better made. He made an effort to talk to her, but he was thinking to himself, with a shudder, 'God in heaven! This is a doll. It's a mother doll. And that's a toy soldier, and there's a daddy doll at home – and this is a Vassily Kashirin doll.'

Any minute now, he felt sure, he would hear the whirr of a motor or the squeak of unoiled wheels. When his mother burst into tears, there was a momentary flash of humanity, but it vanished the moment she spoke, and he was nonplussed and horrified to see water coming from her doll's eyes. Later on, in his cell, when the horror became unbearable, Vassily Kashirin turned to prayer. From all that had passed for religion in his life as a young man in the tradesman's home headed by his father, only a nasty, bitter, disgusting after-taste remained, and there was no faith in it. But at some time, probably in his early childhood, he had heard a short sequence of words which had made him shiver with emotion and had stayed with him throughout his life as a breath of pure poetry. The words were about 'bringing joy to the afflicted'.

So it happened that in his darkest moments he would murmur to himself, 'Joy to the afflicted', without actually praying and with no real understanding, though this lifted his spirits and made him want to go up to some dear person and gently protest about things by saying, 'This life of ours . . . can you call it life? Oh, my dear girl, can you really call it life?'

Then he would suddenly get an urge to fool about, ruffling his hair, dropping down on one knee and offering his breast to be beaten, with a cry of 'Come on, strike me down!'

He never told anyone, not even his closest friends, about his 'Joy to the afflicted', and he seemed to be unaware of it himself, so deeply hidden was it inside him. He rarely brought it back to mind, and when he did it was with wary reluctance.

And now that all the horror of an insoluble mystery had come shockingly visible into his head and swamped him like a spring torrent rushing down a channel to the sea, he felt a sudden urge to pray. He wanted to get down on his knees, but he was too embarrassed to do so in front of the soldier, so he folded his arms across his chest and said in a whisper, 'Joy to the afflicted!'

And in a voice full of anguish and emotion, he repeated himself slowly and clearly: 'Joy to the afflicted, come unto me, give succour to Vaska Kashirin.'

Long ago, while still living it up as a first-year student,

before meeting Werner and joining the society, he had called himself, cockily and pathetically, Vaska Kashirin – and now he felt an urge to use that name again. But those few words, 'Joy to the afflicted!', still rang out with a deathly, hollow ring.

Something had stirred. It was as if a distant image of some gentle and sorrowful figure had come into view, only to fade away gently without lighting up the darkness of impending death. The clock chimed in the tower, dead on time. The soldier in the corridor made a rattling noise that could have come from a sword or gun, and then gave a prodigious yawn with juddering pauses.

'Joy to the afflicted! Why don't you speak? Haven't you got anything to say to Vaska Kashirin?'

He gave a smile full of emotion, and waited. But there was only emptiness, inside and all around him. And the gentle and sorrowful figure did not come back. What did come back to him were needless and painful memories of lighted wax candles, a priest in his robes, a painted icon on the wall, and also the holy father, bending and unbending as he said his prayers and gave his bows, with one eye on Vaska to check that he was praying and not misbehaving. And it all became more ghastly than it had been before the prayer.

Everything had gone.

The madness crept on, unbearable. His mind was fading like the scattered embers of a dying campfire, and cooling like the corpse of a newly dead person with some residual warmth in the heart when the feet and hands have already gone stiff. Once again, with a rush of blood, the fading power of his thought told him that he, Vaska Kashirin, might be going out of his mind here and now, and might experience the kind of suffering for which there was no name, taking him to extremes of pain and agony the like of which no living being had ever known, that he could beat his head against the wall, gouge his own eyes out with a fingernail, say or shout anything that came into his head, weep and swear that he could not take any more of this – and it would mean nothing. Absolutely nothing.

And nothing is what ensued. There were legs down there with a mind and life of their own, still walking about and supporting his shaking, soaking body. There were hands with a mind of their own vainly trying to tighten the smock that kept falling open across his chest, and warm his shaking, soaking body. His body was shivering and freezing. There were eyes still looking. There was something akin to relief in this.

But there was still one shock of pure horror to come: when people walked into his cell. Not getting the message – that the time for his execution had come – he just saw people standing there, and he panicked, almost like a child.

'Not going! Not going!' he murmured inaudibly through deadened lips as he gently withdrew towards the back of the cell, as he had recoiled in childhood when his father had raised his hand.

'Time to get on the road.'

They were saying things, walking about, giving him something. He shut his eyes, swaying a little – and he took his time getting ready to go. It must have meant that his mind was beginning to come back to him when he asked an official for a cigarette. The man politely opened his cigarette-case with its decadent fancy patterning.

10. THE WALLS COME TUMBLING DOWN

The unidentified prisoner known as Werner was a man who had grown weary of living and struggling. There had been a time when he had a great love of life, enjoying the theatre, literature and good company. Endowed with an excellent memory and strong will-power, he had studied several European languages in depth and could easily pass for a German, a Frenchman or an Englishman. He usually spoke German with a Bavarian accent, but he could switch at will and talk like a true-born Berliner. He was a lover of fine clothes and a man of exquisite manners, the only member of his fraternity who dared to appear in high-society ballrooms without risk of being recognized.

But long ago, imperceptibly to his comrades, he had become sardonically disaffected with people at some deep level of the spirit; it was a case of being weighed down by a fatal mixture of desperation and world-weariness. By nature more mathematician than poet, he had had no experience of inspiration or ecstasy, and with every passing minute he felt like a madman trying to square the circle by wading through puddles of human blood. The demon he fought against on a daily basis could not imbue him with self-respect; it was the usual entanglement of stupidity, foul play and falsehood, dirty tricks and filthy deception. The last straw, the thing that seemed to have broken his will to live once and for all, was when he murdered a provocateur on orders from the centre. He did the killing calmly, but after one glance at that dead human face of treachery, now at peace, though also pathetic to look at, he immediately lost all self-respect and belief in his cause. It wasn't a question of sudden remorse; he simply lost every last trace of self-esteem and the slightest interest in himself – he had become insignificant, a tedious irrelevancy. As a man of single-minded, unbreakable will, he stayed on in the organization, ostensibly unchanged, though his eyes had now taken on the glint of something cold and terrible. He said not a word to anyone.

He possessed one other sharply defined quality. Just as there are some people who have never had a headache, so he was a man who had never known fear. And when other people were afraid of something, he looked on this without condemning them, but also without any particular sympathy, as if it was some kind of common ailment that he happened never to have suffered from. He did feel some pity towards his colleagues, especially Vasya Kashirin, but it was a frigid, almost officially sanctioned feeling, something that some of the judges were probably not unfamiliar with.

Werner had realized that execution is not just a matter of dying, but something more. Anyway, he decided to confront it calmly, as if it had no relevance, by living right up to the end as if nothing had happened and nothing was going to happen. This was the only means of expressing his lofty contempt for execution and preserving the last form of inalienable freedom – that of the spirit. Even in court – and this would have been almost unbelievable even to his colleagues, who were fully aware of his capacity for cool detachment and complete disdain – far from thinking about dying or living, he had been calmly working through a difficult game of chess, and this had held his closest and deepest powers of concentration. As a first-rate chess-player, he had launched into this game on the first day of his imprisonment, and had kept it going without interruption. And when he was sentenced to death by hanging, not a single piece was moved on his imaginary board.

Even the fact that he would never be able to finish the game did not stop him, and he started the morning of the last day of his life on earth by going back to put right a rather unsuccessful ploy made the previous day. Squeezing his lowered hands between his knees, he stayed rigid in a sitting position for quite some time, then he got to his feet and began walking about, deep in thought. He had a strange way of walking. Tilting his upper body slightly forwards, he banged down sharply on his heels, so that even on the dry ground his steps rang out with an unmistakable clatter. Softly, only by breathing out, he whistled a little Italian arietta – it helped his thinking.

But this time, for some reason, things went wrong. With an uncomfortable feeling that he had committed a big mistake, even a terrible blunder, he went back on himself several times and checked his game almost from the start. There was no blunder, but the feeling of having made a mistake would not leave him; it grew stronger and more irksome. Then he was struck by an unexpected and offensive idea: maybe the mistake was to use a game of chess to distract his mind from execution and thus protect himself against the fear of death that would seem to be inevitable for a condemned man?

'Hm. Why would I do that?' he responded coldly, and calmly folded the board away. And, with the same degree of close attention that he reserved for the game of chess, like an examination candidate facing a stiff test, he tried to take account of his horrific situation, from which there was no escape. He looked around the room, trying to leave nothing out, worked out how many hours were left before the execution, sketched out an approximate, though reasonably accurate, picture of the execution itself, and then shrugged his shoulders.

'So what's it all about?' he asked of no one in particular, half-questioningly. 'That's all there is to it. Where's the fear in that?'

No, there was nothing to fear. And not only was there nothing to fear, something had been creeping up on him that seemed to be the opposite of what he stood for – a hazy but challenging sensation of enormous joy. And the still-undiscovered mistake no longer seemed so irksome or disappointing; it, too, spoke strongly of something good and quite unexpected, as if he had lost a close friend in death, only to find that he was still alive, sound in wind and limb, and rejoicing.

Werner gave another shrug, and took his own pulse. His heartbeat was up a little, but still strong and regular, a resonant force. Once again, like a new inmate, he took a close look at the walls, the bars, the chair fastened to the floor, and a sudden thought struck him. 'Why am I feeling so easy and happy and free? Especially *free*? When I think about the execution tomorrow, it doesn't seem to be there. When I look at the walls, they don't seem to be there. And I feel so free it's like being on the outside, newly released from a prison that I've been in all my life. What is it all about?'

His hands were beginning to tremble – a new experience for Werner. And his head was more and more filled with furious ideas. It was as if tongues of flame were leaping out inside his head, and the fire had been struggling to get out and shine all over a broad nocturnal landscape that stretched out into the dark distance. And now it was on the outside, and the long-receding landscape was lit up and shining.

Gone was the enervating lassitude that had worn Werner down for the last two years; a clammy, dead-weight serpent with tight-shut eyes and a ghastly pinched-up mouth had fallen away from his heart. In the presence of death, a wonderful youthfulness was being restored to him with its spirit of play. It was something more than wonderful youthfulness. With one of those amazing flashes of spiritual insight that occur to people on rare occasions, raising them to the highest heights of consciousness, Werner suddenly saw life and death brought together, and he was stunned by the splendour of this undreamt-of spectacle. It was like walking along the knife-edge of the highest possible mountain range, seeing life on one side and death on the other in the form of two deep, gorgeous and gleaming seascapes merging at the horizon into a single expanse of infinite space.

'What *is* this? What a heavenly vision!' he said, speaking slowly and automatically raising himself and coming to attention as if he was in the presence of a supreme being. And all things – walls, time and space – were obliterated as he peered with piercing insight into the full depth and breadth of the life that he was leaving.

And life was suddenly different. No longer did he attempt to express what he had seen in words; there were no words in the sparse and meagre resources of human language. Gone for good was the tiny impulse of bitter unpleasantness that used to evoke in him a disdain for other people, and sometimes even a feeling of revulsion at the sight of a human face. It was like a man going up in a hot-air balloon and watching the filthy rubbish of narrow streets disappear as his small town falls away, and ugliness turns into beauty.

Werner walked mechanically over to the table, and leant on it with his right hand. Proud and imperious by nature, he had never struck such a proud, liberated and imperious pose as this, never turned his neck in such a way, or adopted such a glare – because he had never before felt as liberated and imperious as he now did, here in prison just a few hours away from execution and death.

And people were suddenly different; they now looked all pleasant and charming under his newly enlightened gaze. Soaring away beyond time, he could see clearly how young humanity was, only yesterday a beast howling in the forest; and the things that had seemed disgusting in people, horribly unforgivable, had turned into something rather nice – not unlike a toddler's inability to walk properly like an adult, or its babbling chatter filled with sparkling gems of wit, its amusing blunders, slips and painful bruises.

'My dear friends!' Werner gave a sudden, unexpected smile, and instantly lost all the authority of his pose, becoming a prisoner again, suffering the narrowness and discomfort of confinement, increasingly irritated by the intrusively searching eye that stood out against the flatness of the door. And there was something odd: almost instantly he had forgotten what he had been seeing with such sharpness and clarity. Odder still: he made no attempt to recall it. He simply shifted into an easier sitting position, disregarding his usual indifference to bodily discomfort, and with an uncharacteristically feeble and tender smile, nothing like the old Werner grin, he stared at the walls and bars. Then something else occurred that was so unlike Werner it had not happened before: he burst into tears.

'My dear comrades!' he whispered through bitter tears. 'My dear comrades!'

By what secret ways had he travelled from that feeling of pride and limitless freedom to this pathetic display of tenderness and passion? He did not know and didn't even wonder about it. And whether he was simply feeling sorry for those people, his dear comrades, or whether there was something else, something nobler and more impassioned, hidden behind his tears, even this was unknown to his heart, so suddenly resurrected and spring-like.

'My dear comrades! Oh, my dear comrades!'

In this bitterly weeping figure, smiling through his tears, no one would have recognized the cold, aloof, world-weary, arrogant Werner – not the judges, nor his comrades, nor Werner himself.

11. ON THEIR WAY

Before the condemned prisoners were put into their carriages, all five were brought together in a large, cold room with a vaulted ceiling that looked like a disused office or an empty waiting-room. They were allowed to talk among themselves.

But the only one to take immediate advantage of this permission was Tanya Kovalchuk. The others were silently squeezing each other's hands, cold as ice or hot as fire – and silently avoiding eye-contact as they crowded together in an embarrassed little gang with blank faces. Now that they were together again, they were all rather ashamed of what they had been feeling when they were alone, and they were afraid to look at each other, not wanting to see or to display the various, peculiar and rather shameful things they had experienced, or suspected in themselves, as individuals.

But once a couple of glances had been exchanged, they started smiling at each other, and immediately everything felt as natural and easy-going as before; no change had occurred, and if something had occurred, the weight of it was shared between them so equally that it was barely noticeable to each individual. They all spoke and moved about awkwardly, in quick bursts and snatches, or else much too slowly, or too rapidly; sometimes words stuck in throats, and there was much repetition; some sentences were left unfinished or taken as understood, and nobody took any notice. They were all screwing up their eyes and staring at everyday objects with close attention as if they couldn't recognize them, like people used to wearing spectacles who had suddenly taken them off. All of them kept turning around and taking a sharp look behind them, as if someone at their back had called out with something to show them. But this too went unnoticed. Musya and Tanya Kovalchuk had burning cheeks and ears; Sergey had seemed rather pallid at first, but he soon came through it and began to look like his old self.

Vassily was the only one who attracted their attention. Even amongst these people he looked awful, and out of place. This roused Werner to a mixture of sympathy and anxiety, and he spoke to Musya. 'What's wrong with him, Musechka? Is he . . . you know . . . ? We ought to go over and talk to him.'

Vassily gave them a vacant stare, staring at Werner as if he didn't recognize him, and then looking down.

'What have you done to your hair, Vasya, eh? Now, what's all this? Nothing to worry about, brother. Soon be over now. Got to tough it out. That's what we've got to do.'

Vassily did not speak. For a long time it seemed as if he wasn't going to say anything at all, but then a response came, a belated, lifeless sound from terribly far away, like the grave itself reacting to endless calls.

'I'm all right. I will tough it out.' And he repeated: 'I will tough it out.'

85

Werner was delighted to hear it. 'There you are. Good lad. That's the way.'

But he was met by a dark, leaden stare coming from the distant deeps, and an anguished thought flashed across his mind. What was his angle of vision? Where was he coming from when he said things? And, with the deepest sensitivity, he spoke out in sepulchral tones. 'Vasya, listen to me. I love you, very dearly.'

'I love you too.' His leaden answer quavered on the tongue.

Suddenly Musya took hold of Werner's hand, and spoke to him, overplaying her surprise, like an actress on the stage: 'What's this, Werner? You – talking about love? You've *never* talked about love to anybody. Suddenly you're all . . . you know . . . bright-eyed and gentle. What's it all about?'

'What are you getting at?'

And Werner, also overplaying things like an actor, squeezed Musya's hand. 'Yes, I do feel love now. Don't tell on me, please. It's embarrassing. But I do feel love.'

Their eyes met and flashed with brightness while everything around them faded, the way that all other lights are dimmed in a sudden flash of lightning as the intense yellow flame casts a dark shadow on the ground.

'Yes, yes,' said Musya. 'It's all right, Werner.'

'Yes, Musya,' he said. 'Yes, it is.'

Something had passed between them, something understood and firmly established. And Werner's eyes were still flashing when he felt another rush of feeling and strode over to Sergey.

'Seryozha!'

But it was Tanya Kovalchuk who responded. In a trans-
port of delight and on the verge of tears from maternal
pride, she snatched furiously at Sergey's sleeve. 'Werner,'
she said, 'Listen to me. I'm in tears over him. Out of my
mind. And he's doing his exercises.'

'The Müller system?' said Werner with a smile.

Sergey frowned with embarrassment. 'You can laugh,
Werner, but I'm absolutely sure . . .'

They all shared a good laugh. Coming together like this,
and gathering strength in the black fortress, they were
steadily reverting to what they had been before, but they
didn't see this and thought nothing had changed. Suddenly
Werner put a stop to their laughter and spoke to Sergey with
some gravity.

'You're right, Seryozha. Quite right.'

'No, you don't understand,' said Golovin, more cheerfully.
'Of course, we . . .'

But at this point an announcement was made: it was time
to get on the road. And the guards were kind enough to let
them sit together in pairs as they chose. They were indeed
kindness itself, almost too kind, either making a display of
their humanity or else pretending they were not there at all,
and everything was running itself. But they looked pale.

'Musya, you go with him,' said Werner, pointing to
Vassily, who was standing there transfixed.

'I get your meaning.' Musya nodded. 'What about you?'

'Me? Tanya goes with Sergey, and you're with Vasya . . .
I'll be on my own. That's all right. I can cope with that. You
know me.'

Once they were outside, the warm dampness of a dark

night struck them, softly but sharply, straight in the face and eyes, taking their breath away in a gentle, cleansing stream that swept right through their shivering bodies. It was hard to believe that this bewildering feeling came from nothing more than a spring breeze, warm and moist. It was a real spring night, astonishingly beautiful, with a scent of melting snow amid tinkling droplets in the boundless empty space. Tumbling showers of rapid raindrops busily chased each other down, pitter-pattering in the close harmony of song until one of them lost the beat and the whole thing collapsed into the muddle of a happy fandango. After that, a big strong raindrop would set up a new beat, and off went the pitter-patter into another fast spring song, neatly and resonantly performed. And a pale glow from the electric lights shone down on the town, and the fortress roofs.

'O-oh!' Sergey Golovin took a deep breath and held it, as if reluctant to let such lovely fresh air out of his lungs.

'How long has the weather been like this?' Werner wanted to know. 'It's just like spring.'

'Only a couple of days.' The response was obligingly polite. 'But we still get bad frosts.'

One by one the dark carriages were brought up. Each of them accepted two passengers before trundling off into the darkness towards a lantern swinging at the gates. Each was surrounded by the grey silhouettes of guards, and the horses' hooves rang out, clattering on the road surface or slithering through the wet snow.

Just as Werner bent down to get into his carriage, one of the guards made a casual observation: 'Somebody else travelling with you.'

Werner was taken aback. 'Where to? Where's he going? What do you mean – somebody else?'

The guard said nothing. Sure enough, something small and still but obviously alive was squashed into a dark corner of the carriage, as he could see from an angled shaft of light from a lantern that picked out the glint of an open eye. In the process of getting into his seat, Werner bumped against somebody's knee.

'Sorry, my friend.'

There was no response. It was only when the carriage had started to roll forward that he asked a question in halting Russian, with a stammer. 'Who . . . who are you . . . ?'

'My name is Werner. Sentenced to death by hanging for the attempted assassination of N.N. Who are you?'

'Er, Yanson. Not to hang me.'

Here they were, riding along a couple of hours from facing the huge, inscrutable mystery of passing over from life to death, and they had just met. Life and death were operating together in two simultaneous planes, but life was still life, down to the silliest laughable details.

'What did you do, Yanson?'

'Stabbed my boss. Killed him. For the money.'

To judge by his voice, Yanson seemed half-asleep. Werner found his limp hand in the darkness and gave it a squeeze. Yanson extracted his hand just as feebly.

'Are you feeling scared?' asked Werner.

'I don't want.'

Neither of them spoke. Werner found the Estonian's hand again and gave it a strong squeeze between his own two dry, burning-hot palms. It lay there, lifeless and stiff as a bit of board, and Yanson no longer tried to withdraw it.

It was cramped and stuffy in the carriage; there was a smell of soldiers' clothes, stale air, manure and sodden boot-leather. A junior guard was sitting across from Werner, and his hot breath reeked of onions and cheap tobacco. But there were a few cracks through which pungent fresh air made its way into this stuffy little box on wheels, and this was more spring-like than outside. The carriage lurched right and left, and even seemed to turn back on itself; sometimes it gave an impression of circling for hours on end without moving from one spot. To begin with, a bluish electric light shone in through the thick blinds which had been lowered over the windows, then suddenly, following one particularly sharp turn, it went slightly darker, this being the only means of guessing that they had turned off into the godforsaken streets of the outskirts and were getting close to the S— railway terminal. Now and again, at sharp turns, Werner's bent knee, still living, bumped chummily against the guard's living bent knee, and execution was a hard thing to believe in.

'Where are we going?' Yanson suddenly asked.

His head was spinning a little from the constant twisting and turning of the dark box, and he felt slightly sick.

Werner gave his answer, and squeezed the Estonian's hand all the harder. He felt like saying something particularly friendly and affectionate to this sleepy little man, and he felt a greater love for him than for anyone ever before.

'My dear friend! You don't look too comfortable sitting like that. Come a bit closer.'

Yanson was quiet for a moment, and then gave his response. 'No, thanks. I'm all right. You going to be hung?'

'Yes!' Werner answered in a surprisingly cheerful tone, almost laughing, and he waved his hand casually, almost exaggeratedly relaxed, as if this was a laughing matter, some silly trick that nice people with a terrible sense of humour wanted to play on him.

'You married?' asked Yanson.

'Oh no. No wife for me. I'm on my own.'

'I'm not . . . not married, I mean,' said Yanson, correcting himself after a bit of thought.

By now, even Werner's head was beginning to swim. And as the minutes went by it seemed more and more as if they were on their way to some kind of celebration. It is a strange fact that almost all people on their way to execution have had this feeling; along with all the anguish and terror, they have a vague sense of enjoying the bizarre event that was about to take place. Reality runs away with fantasy, and death joins forces with life to create new visions. It seemed quite likely that bunting would have been put out for them.

'Here we are,' said Werner cheerily, looking up with new interest, when the carriage stopped, and he nipped out smartly. But Yanson was taking his time. Saying nothing, but holding onto things with a feeble grip, he refused to get out. When he took hold of a handle, the guard had no trouble in loosening the lifeless fingers and prising his hand free; when he took hold of a corner, the door, one of the tall wheels, he was eased away from them by a guard who hardly had to exert himself. He hadn't really got hold of these things; the uncommunicative Yanson was simply sticking sleepily to anything that came to hand, and he was quickly and effortlessly pulled away. At last he was out and on his feet.

There was no bunting. It was night-time, and the station was dark, deserted and lifeless. It was too early for the passenger trains to be running, and the silent train that awaited these passengers needed neither bright lights nor ceremony. And suddenly Werner felt bored with the whole thing. Not troubled by fear, but bored out of his mind and wearied by a hugely oppressive sense of tedium which made him want to go away somewhere and lie down with his eyes tight shut, Werner stretched himself and gave a prodigious yawn. Yanson followed him by stretching and giving a series of quick, short yawns.

'Let's get it over and done with!' said Werner wearily. Yanson, with nothing to say, shrank into himself.

While the condemned prisoners were moving down the deserted platform, which had been cordoned off by soldiers, towards dimly lit carriages, Werner fetched up alongside Sergey Golovin, who pointed to one side and started talking, though only one thing was audible – the word 'lantern' – and even that was swallowed up in a great long and weary yawn.

'What do you mean?' asked Werner with an answering yawn.

'That lantern. The lamp inside – it's smoking,' said Sergey.

Werner turned and looked at it: sure enough, the lamp inside the lantern was giving off thick smoke, and the glass panels were blackening at the top.

'Yes, it is.'

And a sudden thought occurred to him. 'Why on earth should I be bothered if the lamp's smoking, when . . .' The same thing had evidently occurred to Sergey; he glanced at Werner, and looked away. But both of them had stopped yawning.

All seven were heading for the carriages, and only Yanson needed to be taken by the arms. First, he had dragged his feet as if the soles of his shoes were sticking to the wooden platform, then he had bent his knees and hung in mid-air, held up by the guards, or dragged his legs like a drunk, with his socks scraping the boards. It took some time to get him in through the door, though he wasn't speaking.

Vassily Kashirin got along on his own, but only by vaguely copying his friends – what they did, he did. But as he stepped through onto the carriage floor, he stumbled, and the guard took his arm to steady him, at which Vassily shuddered and gave a great roar as he shoved the hand away. 'Aaargh!'

'What's up, Vasya?' said Werner, moving in quickly.

Vassily said nothing. He was shaking all over. The guard, embarrassed and rather offended, explained himself.

'I was only trying to help, but he . . .'

'Come on, Vasya, I'll give you a hand,' said Werner, trying to take his arm. But once again Vassily shoved the hand away, and his roar was even louder. 'Aaargh!'

'Vasya, it's me, Werner.'

'I know. Leave me alone. I can manage.'

Still shaking, he got in on his own, and sat down in a corner of the carriage. Bending down towards Musya,

Werner signalled with his eyes and spoke softly to her. 'What do you make of that?'

'Not good,' she answered just as softly. 'He's already dead. Werner, is death real?'

'I don't know, Musya. I don't think so,' said Werner, serious-minded and thoughtful.

'I thought you'd say that. But him? He wore me out in the carriage. Like riding with a corpse.'

'I don't know, Musya. Maybe death is real for some people. Just for a while. Then, afterwards, it won't be. Death's been real with me, but it isn't now.'

Musya's rather pallid cheeks flushed red. '*Been real*, Werner? Been?'

'It's been, and gone. Same for you.'

There was a racket at the carriage door. All banging heels, noisy breathing and reckless spitting, in came Gypsy Mike. He cast his eyes around, and stood his ground.

'No room in here, guard!' he shouted to the worn-out guard who was watching him resentfully. 'Give me some room, or I'm not going. You can hang me here on a lamp-post. And that damn carriage, you bastards! Call that a carriage? Devil's shit, that's what it was!'

But then, suddenly, he lowered his head, stuck his neck out and walked in like that to be with the others. Framed by a wild shock of hair and beard, his piercing black eyes glared at them, on the brink of insanity. 'Hello there, gentlemen! There we have it, then! Good morning, sir!'

Nudging Werner, he sat down across from him. Then, lowering his head into close proximity, he winked at him and flashed a hand across his neck. 'You too, eh?'

'Yes,' said Werner with a smile.

'All of 'em?'

'Yes.'

'Aha!' Gypsy Mike gave a grin, and his eyes quickly probed them all, lingering for a while on Musya and Yanson. He winked again at Werner. 'That minister?'

'Yes. What about you?'

'I, sir, am here on special business. No time for ministers! I, sir, am a villain, that's what I am. A killer. Don't you worry, sir. Come a bit closer. I'm not here in your company because I want to be. Plenty of room for us all in the world to come.'

Then, from under his tousled mass of hair, his wild eyes swept across them all in one swift, suspicious stare. They returned his look without comment, but seriously and with evident sympathy. He gave another grin and several times he tapped Werner on the knee. 'There you have it, sir. Like in that song: "Mother oak-tree, oh so green, make no sound for me . . ."'

'Why do you keep calling me *sir*, when . . . ?'

'That's right,' agreed Gypsy Mike with some satisfaction. 'How can you be a sir when you're going to hang next to me? Now that man's a sir,' he continued, pointing to the silent guard. 'But that one of your lot is no worse than us.' His eyes had picked out Vassily. 'Sir . . . you're scared too, aren't you, sir?'

'Not too bad,' came the answer, dragged out thickly from a stiff tongue.

'What do you mean "not too bad"? Don't be ashamed. No need to be ashamed. Only a dog wags its tail and grins

95

at you when it's going to be hung, and you're a man, aren't you? And who's that with the big long ears? Not one of yours, is he?'

His eyes kept darting about, and he was constantly slurping on sweet saliva as it welled up, and spitting it out. Yanson, who had squeezed himself into a rigid lump in the corner, slightly stirred the flaps on his fur cap, but he didn't say anything.

'Killed his boss.'

'Good God!' said Gypsy Mike in some surprise. 'Do they really let blokes like him go around killing people?'

Gypsy Mike had been furtively eyeing Musya for some time, and now he suddenly rounded on her, staring hard and straight. 'You, missy. How are you mixed up in this, missy? Look, she's gone all pink, and she's laughing. Look, she is, you know.' He grabbed Werner by the knee, and his clutching fingers exerted a grip of iron. 'Look at her. *Look*.'

Blushing a little and with a tiny smile of embarrassment, Musya stared straight into his piercing, half-crazy eyes with their wild and wearily pleading look.

Nobody spoke.

The busy wheels drummed on, and the tiny carriages rocked on their narrow railway, going flat out. When the little engine came to a bend or a crossing, it gave a shrill, keen whistle, the driver not wanting to run over anybody. And it was barbarous to think that such a degree of routine human effort and efficiency should be applied to the hanging of people, and that the craziest deed on earth was being done in such a simple and rational manner. On went the carriages, with the people sitting there as they always do, travelling like normal travellers, waiting, as always, for the next stop. 'This train will halt for five minutes.'

After that comes death – eternity – the great mystery.

12. JOURNEY'S END

On went the little carriages, flat out.

Sergey Golovin had lived for several years with his parents in a house on this very route; he had travelled it by day and night, and he knew it well. If he closed his eyes it was easy to imagine that he was now on his way home; he had stayed late with friends in town and had caught the last train.

'Not long now,' he said, opening his eyes and peering out through the uncommunicatively dark window and its protective grille.

Nobody stirred or responded; only Gypsy Mike did anything, and he was spitting out gobbets of saliva. He began to give his eyes a free run of the carriage, taking in the walls and feeling at the windows, the doors, the soldiers.

''S cold,' said Vassily Kashirin through tight lips that seemed literally frozen. It came out as ''S co-o—'

Tanya Kovalchuk was fumbling with something. 'Here's a scarf. Tie it around your neck. It's very warm.'

'Round his *neck*?' asked Sergey to everyone's surprise, and he was shocked by his own question.

But since everybody was thinking the same thing, nobody

heard it, as if no one had spoken or they had all said the same thing at the same time.

'Never mind, Vasya. Wrap yourself up. Wrap up warm,' was Werner's advice, then he turned to Yanson and spoke to him in a kindly voice. 'My dear friend, you must be feeling the cold.'

'Werner, maybe he wants a smoke. Listen, my friend, do you fancy a smoke?' asked Musya. 'We've got fags.'

'Oh, yes.'

'Give him a cigarette, Seryozha,' said Werner, perking up.

But Sergey was already getting one out. And they all looked on with affection as Yanson's fingers accepted the cigarette, the match flared and a stream of deep-blue smoke issued from Yanson's mouth.

'Oh, thanks,' said Yanson. 'That's nice.'

'Very funny thing,' said Sergey.

'What's funny? asked Werner, turning towards him. 'What's funny about that?'

'Well – just this cigarette.' He was holding the cigarette, an ordinary cigarette, in his ordinary, living fingers, and staring at it in amazement, as if he was transfixed with horror. And they all turned their eyes onto that thin little tube, watching as a ribbon of blue smoke curled up from the end to be blown away by their breath, and the ash built up and went dark. It went out.

'It's gone out,' said Tanya.

'Yes, it has.'

'To hell with it!' said Werner, scowling anxiously at Yanson, whose hand looked dead as it drooped down, still holding his cigarette. Suddenly Gypsy Mike whipped round and leaned across, bringing his face right up to Werner's and rolling the whites of his eyes like a horse as he whispered to him. 'Shall we get one of them guards, sir, eh? 'ave a little go?'

'Don't do that,' said Werner, also in a whisper. 'Just take what's coming to you.'

'What for? Bit of fun, 'avin' a scrap, eh? I gives 'im one, 'e does me, and you don't know when you've 'ad it. As if you wasn't dead at all.'

'No, don't do it,' said Werner, turning to Yanson. 'Why aren't you smoking, my friend?'

Suddenly Yanson's flabby face crumpled pathetically. It was as if someone had pulled a string that worked his face, and his wrinkles had all criss-crossed each other. And he seemed to be half-asleep as he started whimpering, without shedding any tears, in a voice that was dry as dust, almost like play-acting. 'Don't feel like smoking. Aargh! Aargh! Aargh! Nobody not to hang me. Aargh! Aargh! Aargh!'

Things were going on around him. With tears streaming down her face, Tanya Kovalchuk stroked his sleeve, straightened the sagging flaps of his tattered cap and spoke to him. 'My lovely little man! Please don't cry, my dear little boy! I know how unhappy you are!'

Musya looked away. Gypsy Mike caught her eye and gave one of his grins. 'Funny chap, his honour. Drinks tea with the rest of us, but he's got a chill in his belly,' he said with a bit of a laugh. But his own face had turned a blue-black colour, and it looked like cast-iron. His big yellow teeth were chattering.

Then the little carriages jolted and noticeably slowed down. Everybody except Yanson and Kashirin rose up in their seats, and then, just as quickly, sat back down again.

'Our stop!' said Sergey.

All the air seemed to have been sucked out of the carriage, it was so hard to breathe. Swelling hearts threatened to burst through the walls of their chests, blocking throats, thumping wildly and screaming from terror in voices coursing with blood. All eyes were cast down at the shuddering floor; all ears followed the sound of wheels going round and round, slower and slower, skidding, going round again, then – coming to a sudden stop.

The train had halted.

Then the dream-world took over. Not that it was all that terrifying; it was a ghost-world, mind-bendingly weird and alien, with the dreamer himself left out of things and only his bodiless shade moving about, speaking without sound and agonizing without agony. They were sleepwalking their way out of the carriage, forming up in pairs and drinking in the woodland air with all its special springtime freshness. Yanson was dumbly sleepwalking as he put up a show of feeble resistance, only to be forcibly ejected from the carriage without a word.

They dropped down from the little steps.

'Are we walking it?' someone asked, almost cheerily.

'Not far to go,' said someone else, just as cheerily.

Then they set off in a large, black group of silent people, walking through woodland down a badly maintained road in all the gentle springtime dampness. Bracing air blew at them fresh from the woods; it was slippery underfoot and when they ran into deeper snow, hands reached out instinctively for a companion. Heavy breathing came from the escorting guards, who were having a tough time struggling through nothing but deep snow. A voice spoke out angrily. 'They might have cleared the road. Fancy leaving us to muck about in this lot!'

Someone else put in an apologetic explanation. 'They did clear it, sir. Can't do nothing about the thaw, though.'

Consciousness was coming back, but only partly, in odd little bits and pieces. A moment's sensible thought confirmed it.

'That's right. They couldn't possibly have cleared the road.'

Then everything started to fade away again, leaving nothing but a sense of smell, the unbearably pungent aroma of air, woodland and melting snow, and the next moment everything stood out with unbelievable clarity – the woods, the night, the roadway, and the fact that they were on their way to being hanged – any minute now, straightaway. The snatches of whispered talk were strained and desultory.

'Soon be four o'clock.'

'I said we were leaving early.'

'Gets light at five.'

'Yes, it does. Ought to have . . .'

It was still dark when they stopped in an open space. Not far ahead was a thin patch of trees that could be seen through because it was winter, and there you could see two silent lanterns bobbing about. And the gallows.

'I've lost one of my galoshes,' said Sergey Golovin.

'You what?' said Werner, not getting his idea.

'I've lost one of my galoshes. It's cold.'

'Where's Vassily got to?'

'Don't know. Oh, that's him over there.'

It was Vassily, a dark, motionless figure.

'What about Musya?'

'I'm here. Is that you, Werner?'

They were now taking a good look around, though avoiding the place where the lanterns were bobbing about with a horrific meaning that was only too clear. To their left, the bare woods seemed to have thinned out, allowing a huge, smooth, white shape to stare through at them, and a wet wind to blow.

'It's the sea,' said Sergey Golovin, sniffing the air and tasting it in his mouth. 'That's the sea.'

Musya's response was sonorously poetic. 'My love is wider than the open sea . . .'

'What's all that about, Musya?'

'My love is wider than the open sea, unbounded by the shore-line of our lives . . .'

'My love is wider than the open sea . . .' Sergey repeated the words pensively, succumbing to the voice, the sounds, the words.

'My love is wider than the open sea . . .' Werner repeated them too, then suddenly a thrill of delight took him by surprise. 'Muska, you're still such a young thing!'

Close upon him, straight into Werner's ear, came an urgent, gasping whisper from Gypsy Mike: 'Sir, listen. Sir. Look at them woods, eh? What the hell is that? Them lanterns over there. See? Is that where they does the 'anging? What is it?'

Werner took a look. Gypsy Mike was in a desperate state, aware of his impending death.

'We should start saying goodbye . . .' said Tanya Kovalchuk.

'Hang on, they've still got to read out the sentence,' said Werner. 'What's happened to Yanson?'

Yanson was lying in the snow, and there were people nearby, seeing to him. There was a sudden strong whiff of ammonia.

'What's holding you up, doctor? Nearly ready?' The question sounded impatient.

'It's all right. He's only fainted. Wipe his ears with snow. Look, he's coming round. You can start the reading.'

Light from a hidden lantern fell across a document held in white, ungloved hands. Document and hands were all a bit shaky, as was the voice.

'Gentlemen, shall we do without the reading? I think you all know what it says. What do you think?'

'Don't read it,' said Werner, answering for them all, and the little lantern went out.

They also refused the services of a priest, and a large, black silhouette slipped away silently into the depths of darkness. Dawn seemed to be coming up; the snow looked a little whiter than before, the bodies a little darker, as the woods thinned out, taking on a more ordinary, yet more pathetic, appearance.

'Gentlemen, you must walk on in twos. Please pair off as you wish, but I must ask you to get a move on.'

Werner pointed to Yanson, who was back on his feet, supported by two guards. 'I'll go with him. Seryozha, you take Vassily. Off you go.'

'Right.'

'Are we going together, Musechka?' asked Kovalchuk. 'Come on. Give us a kiss.'

Kisses were rapidly exchanged. Gypsy Mike's kiss was heavy – you could feel his teeth; Yanson's was soft and limp,

103

with his mouth half-open – he didn't seem to know what he was doing. When Sergey Golovin and Kashirin had taken a few steps, Kashirin came to a sudden stop and called out loud and clear, in a strange voice that didn't belong to him: 'Bye, comrades!'

'Bye, comrades!' came the answering call.

They walked off. It was now calm. The little lanterns through the trees had stopped bobbing about. They were expecting to hear a scream, a voice, some kind of noise – but it was just as calm up ahead and the little lanterns, now still, gave off a yellow gleam.

'Oh, good God!' came a wild, hoarse cry from one of them. They looked round. It was Gypsy Mike, still in his desperate condition with death now upon him. 'They've started hanging them!'

They recoiled, and all was calm again. Gypsy Mike showed his desperation by clutching at the air. 'This isn't right! I ask you, gentlemen – me, all on my own? More fun with a bit of company, gentlemen. *It's not right!*'

He grabbed Werner by the arm, his fingers squeezing tight and then relaxing as if it was some sort of game. 'You, sir. My dear friend. Let me go with you. Please . . . Don't say no.'

Werner agonized over his reply. 'I can't, my friend. I'm with him.'

'Oh, my God! So, I'm on my own, am I? It's not right, is it? *Gentlemen!*'

Musya took a step forward, and spoke softly. 'Come on. You come with me.'

Gypsy Mike recoiled with a wild glare, rolling the whites of his eyes. 'You?'

'Yes.'

'Look at you . . . slip of a girl . . . aren't you scared? Might be better off on my own. Forget it.'

'No, I'm not scared.'

He gave his wide grin. 'Look at you . . . and I'm a real villain . . . you must be feeling queasy . . . If you are, I'd be better on my own. Won't hold it against you.'

Musya said nothing. In the thin light of early dawn, her face looked pale and mysterious. Then she went straight up to Gypsy Mike, put both hands around his neck and gave him a firm kiss on the lips. He took her by the shoulders with his fingers, pushed her away at arm's length, and gave her another shake. Then, slobbering out loud with emotion, he kissed her on the lips, nose and eyes.

'Come on, then!'

Suddenly the nearest soldier seemed to reel back, and his hands opened up, dropping his gun. But instead of bending down to pick it up, he stood still and hesitated for a moment, made a sharp turn and ran off like a blind man towards the woods and the untrodden snow.

'Where are you off to?' whispered his fellow soldier, frightened. 'Stop!'

But the first man kept on, wading silently through the deep snow. He must have tripped over something because then he fell face-down in the snow with his arms flailing. He just lay there.

'Pick your gun up, bird-brain, or I'll do it for you,' said Gypsy Mike ominously. 'Don't you know what duty is?'

The little lanterns were busy again. Werner and Yanson were next in line.

'Goodbye, sir,' said Gypsy Mike in a loud voice. 'We'll know each other in the next world. Don't ignore me when you see me. And bring me a drink of water. It's hot where I'm going.'

'Goodbye.'

'I don't want,' said Yanson.

But Werner took him by the hand, and the Estonian managed a few steps on his own before ostentatiously coming to a halt and throwing himself down on the snow. They bent over him, pulled him to his feet and carried him along; he put up only a feeble struggle against the hands that were holding him. Why wasn't he screaming? He had probably forgotten that he still had a voice.

Again the little lanterns with their yellow light stopped all movement.

'Oh well, Musechka, that means I'm on my own,' said Tanya Kovalchuk sadly. 'We've lived together, but here we are . . .'

'Tanechka, my dear friend . . .'

But Gypsy Mike made an emotional intervention. Holding Musya's hand, as if he was frightened of her being taken away from him, he spoke quickly, spelling things out. 'Oh miss, you can manage on your own. You're a pure soul. You can go wherever you want without anybody else. Do you see? *I can't*. I'm a villain . . . know what I mean? I can't do it on my own. They're going to say, "You're a murderer – where do you think you're off to?" I've done the lot – even horse-stealing, for God's sake. But going with her . . . well, it's like being with a child. See what I mean?'

'Yes, I do see. Go on then . . . Musechka, one last kiss . . .'

'Yes, don't forget the kissing,' Gypsy Mike said, encouraging the two women. 'It's your thing. Got to say goodbye, and get it right.'

Musya and Gypsy Mike moved off together. She, the woman, proceeded with great care, holding her skirts off the ground as always; he, the man, kept tight hold of her, moving forward cautiously, feeling the way with his foot as he walked her to her death.

The lights had stopped moving. Tanya Kovalchuk was surrounded by empty silence. The soldiers kept quiet – grey figures in the soft, uncoloured light of early day.

'I'm the only one left,' said Tanya suddenly, with a sigh. 'Seryozha's dead. Werner's dead, and Vassily. Only me left. Soldier boys, all soldier boys, and me on my own. Only me to go . . .'

The sun was coming up over the sea.

The bodies were carefully stowed in boxes. And driven away. With their elongated necks, savagely bulging eyes and swollen blue tongues protruding like ghastly, unidentifiable flowers from lips flecked with bloody foam, the corpses came cruising back along the road they had followed when they had walked there, still alive. And the springtime snow was just as soft and scented; and the springtime air was just as fresh and keen. One black thing stood out in the snow, wet and trampled – Sergey's lost galosh.

And this was how people welcomed the rising sun.

1908